MARRIED TO NUMBER 22

GRIZZLIES HOCKEY #1

ELISE FABER

MARRIED TO NUMBER TWENTY-TWO
BY ELISE FABER

MARRIED TO NUMBER TWENTY-TWO
Copyright © 2025 Elise Faber
Print ISBN-13: 978-1-63749-155-3
Ebook ISBN-13: 978-1-63749-154-6

GRIZZLIES HOCKEY

Married to Number Twenty-Two
Divorced from Number Thirty-Eight
Knocked Up by Number Ninety

ONE

Aiden

I wake up to a heavy knock on my condo's front door and glare blearily at my phone in the charger.

"Two in the fucking morning," I mutter, grabbing a pillow and clamping it over my ears. "It's two o'clock in the morning on my fucking birthday, and I have to deal with this shit."

This *shit* being my neighbors.

It's not the first time they've pounded drunk on my door, desperate for their roommate to let them in to what they think is their condo.

This was sort of funny the first time.

I remember those days, drinking too much, being dumb.

But after the second and the third—where I gained status into the inner circle and a code to the keypad to their apartment door—it was no longer cute.

Now, six months and countless times of bailing them out later, I'm so not in the mood.

Especially when it's my fucking birthday.

The knocking cuts off and I think—pray—that they've gotten the hint.

But it's approximately two seconds later when it starts up again.

I glance at my phone again, see that really five minutes have passed, making it two-seventeen and officially my twenty-fifth birthday.

Some present.

Twenty-five years old and...still living next to a bevy of drunk morons.

Yup. Pro hockey player. Single. Relatively good-looking. And *still* dealing with annoying drunk frat boys.

I'm living the life.

Fucking hell. I need to buy a house, get away from neighbors above and below and on all sides of me.

But that's a tomorrow Aiden problem.

Tonight it's weighing answering the door, shuttling the dumbasses to their apartment across the hall, or clamping another pillow over my head and hoping for the best.

The first is annoying. And necessary.

Mostly because the second is just annoying. Ignoring the knocking only means extending the torture. They won't give up, not now that they've begun, not now that I've been the person seeing them home when they're drunk and disoriented (and disorderly, really) over the last half year.

So really, it's less choice and more...an annoying necessity.

Sighing, I toss back the blankets and stomp to my apartment door, whipping it open to reveal...

Not Benny, the messiest of the frat boy quad from across the hall.

But rather...a slender brunette.

She's standing on my doorstep and her gaze drops from

mine, sliding down my body in a slow perusal. "Ho, mama," she whispers.

Jesus Christ, it only gets worse.

And even more worse because the dragging of her gray eyes —gray eyes that seem semi-familiar—has my cock twitching.

What the fuck is wrong with me?

I shake myself, tighten my hold on the edge of the door, preparing to slam it closed and ask, "Who the fuck are you?"

Her smile doesn't falter as she says, "It's me." But as I stare at her, not recognizing who *me* is, the edges of her mouth wilt just the slightest bit. "It's Luna," she whispers.

I continue to watch her uncomprehendingly.

"From Rockfield?" she adds.

Recognition begins to dawn, and I know why her eyes seemed so familiar. "Luna Maybelle?"

"Yes!" Relief dancing across her face. "That's me." She nods, grinning again, and I see it then, the smile that belonged to my best friend and first love. God, how could I *not* instantly recognize it? We spent hours and hours together inside our childhood rink, hanging out in between my practices and her figure skating training. And we spent time outside it too— mostly at my place, the chaos of my big family something she seemed to crave almost to obsession.

Probably because, aside from her grandmother, she only had her brother and father in her life, and her father was an asshole—and her brother an asshole in training.

But that's not the point.

Luna is here now.

Luna Maybelle. The first girl I ever lusted after, ever kissed. Ever *loved*.

I see that Luna now in her smile—the mischief and brightness, the joy for life and wicked sense of humor.

But she's not little Luna anymore.

Christ, she's anything but—tall, beautiful, curves for days—and she's staring at me.

Because *I'm* staring at her.

Fucking hell.

I spur myself into motion.

"Luna! Oh my God!" I pull her into a hug. "What the hell are you doing here?"

"It's your birthday!" She holds up a piece of paper that looks faintly familiar. "And, well, it's mine too, remember?"

That's right.

We have the same birthday.

"We're both twenty-five, single, and—"

My eyes narrow in on the paper. It's crumpled and stained, as though it's years old.

A purple and pink swirl decorates the edges and suddenly I remember her painstakingly drawing it as we sat side-by-side at one of the high top tables of the ice rink, waiting for the Zamboni to finish cutting the ice.

Her brow had been furrowed. Her movements carefully controlled.

And I had been obsessing over how pink her lips were and what her butt looked like in her skating dress, so much so that I barely remember what we'd been drawing.

No, I think hard, grabbing on to those memories, not what *we'd* been drawing.

The *contract* we'd put together.

The contract my hormonal thirteen-year-old self had signed.

With a sparkly pink colored pencil.

A giant boulder settles in my stomach, but before I can snap myself out of the horror of those memories, she shoves the paper in my hands then throws her arms around my neck.

"We're getting married!"

TWO

Luna

MY HEART IS POUNDING and pretty much every cell in my body is telling me to stop this insanity and to turn around and get the hell out of here.

To leave Aiden to his life without adding the craziness of mine.

But I'm desperate.

And alone.

And this is the only thing that's given me the slightest bit of hope over the last eight months.

And...because I'm almost out of time.

So, I reach into the paper bag I brought, pull out the over-sized grocery store cupcake I bought with pretty much the last money I had in my account.

Pretty much because I still technically have nine dollars and sixty-seven cents left until pay day.

Part of that desperate.

But not *all* of it.

Because I can manage the money—yeah, I've been living paycheck to paycheck, surviving because I don't have access to the family funds I'm legally entitled to, but I have a job and a car and a place to live.

I'm lucky.

And I'm...still almost out of time with very limited ways to move forward.

"Luna," he says and the note of warning, of sharpness in his voice—Aiden was the one person who never disappointed me, who never hurt me—stings.

Slamming the door on those thoughts, I drop the bag to the floor, fumble with the lid of the plastic box of the cupcake, managing to get it open just before I hear him say, "Luna," again. Only this time, instead of censure, his tone has gone gentle.

Right. I can't have that either.

Gentle is soft. Soft means that I'll have all those same feelings again.

And then the Maybelle curse will strike anew.

I shove all that down as I hold up the cupcake, slap a bright smile on my face, one that I perfected during my competition days, and declare, "Happy Birthday!"

Then watch a strange cascade of emotions fly across his face—disbelief and confusion, sadness and pleasure, and...a softness.

A tenderness.

Like a store-bought cupcake and a middle-of-the-night declaration is so far away from what he was expecting to receive that it means more than it should.

I ignore the blip in my heart.

"Luna," he says a third time.

And *this* time it sends heat flickering through me, twining down through my belly, dancing between my thighs.

Uh-oh.

Shaking myself, I march across the room, set the cupcake on the counter, and pull out the lighter and candles I bought, further depleting my bank account.

Thank God, payday is Friday.

Which is in far too many days, if my stomach has any say.

But don't all those health nuts preach about fasting?

It's good for me, right?

Meanwhile, I ignore the rumbling in my stomach saying that it may be good for me but that doesn't mean it's fun, and plop the "2" and "5" candles into the top of the cake.

"This is crazy, Luns."

My heart skips at the nickname, and my stomach twists at the words.

Because he's the only one who ever called me that.

And because he's right.

This *is* crazy.

But...desperate times and desperate measures.

Plus, a bit—or *more*—of impulsivity that will likely blow up in my face thrown in.

I flick the lighter, sparking the little flame to life, holding it over the first wick until it catches then the second. "Happy Birthday," I say quietly, nudging it toward him, finally finding the courage to truly look at him.

He's gorgeous.

He was when we were teenagers and he's even more so now. A boy grown into a man—no longer a body built on lean strength and wiry prowess, but instead he's all broad shoulders and a flat stomach and thighs that are so powerful my mind drifts to all the naughty things that brawn could be used for.

But it's when he turns, bends, and picks up a pillow that must have fallen off his couch at some point—whether by my buzzing about and acting like a frenzied hummingbird or earlier in the day before I intruded on his peace, I don't know. But it's his turning and bending that has my body going stock still for a second.

His ass.

God, his ass.

Why is it that hockey players always have the best asses?

He straightens and I jerk my gaze away, realize the candles are burning down, sending wax onto the swirls of frosting that were making my stomach hungry in a completely different way, and say, "Come make a wish."

There's a flicker of something across his striking green eyes, something intense that I can't read.

But then he's slowly striding toward me, expression inscrutable.

One hand hits the counter. Then the other.

He leans forward, lips pursed—something that sends another flare of heat through my belly—and starts to blow.

"Wait!"

He freezes aside from those green eyes.

They slide toward mine, hold.

"You didn't make a wish."

He didn't have time, just walked over and started to blow.

He lifts a brow in question.

"It's your birthday," I whisper, heart pounding. I don't know why this is so important to me right now—or maybe I do, but I just don't want to look that closely at the emotions churning their way through my insides. Either way, I keep whispering, "You have to make a wish before you blow out the candles."

Green eyes fixing mine in place.

A big body next to mine, the power in his frame coiled tightly, as though it may spring free at any moment.

Then his eyes close, he's statue still for a heartbeat.

His lids peel back...

And he blows.

THREE

Aiden

MAKE A WISH.

Make a wish.

If she knew the thought that crossed my mind, so close to my teenage fantasies, to this gorgeous woman with curves for days who positively vibrates with brightness and energy—despite it being the middle of the night—she'd likely be high-tailing it to the door.

Or maybe not, considering she was the one who showed up to my condo, a marriage contract in hand.

She shifts slightly and my eyes fly open, a curl of worry slicing through me.

Is she going to disappear just as quickly as she appeared?

Flit back out of my life like this is a bizarre dream and I'll wake up in a couple of hours, hockey on the brain, a job to do...

Alone.

But I'm not alone now.

I can hear her, smell her, *want* her.

I blow out the candles, watch her stormy gray eyes warm, as though the sun is peeking through thunderclouds, beams of light illuminating the sky.

Beautiful.

"Great!" she exclaims, startling me and I jerk myself out of my thoughts.

Before I can say anything to make this interaction make sense, she turns away, starts opening drawers, the noises of one flying open and then slamming closed then another and another making me jump.

"Um," I begin.

Begin because anything I was going to say is cut off by another *crash*.

"Luna—"

Another drawer opens. Then closes.

"I—"

"Found it!" she exclaims, holding up a fork. Then her brows pull together, an adorable vee forming that I want to press my lips to, want to smooth away with my thumb. "Is there a reason your utensils are next to your cleaning supplies? That seems like an accidental poisoning waiting to happen."

Right.

I'm not really up for a conversation regarding my utensil placement at three in the morning.

But if this Luna is the same Luna I grew up with a decade ago bringing that—albeit logical—point up, me trying to explain that my moving in just consisted of me dumping shit in random drawers isn't going to fly. Pretty soon we'll be reorganizing my kitchen and distracting her from that task will be a lesson in futility.

Once she gets something into her head, she's like a dog to a bone.

A really big, really tasty bone.

I don't have a battle in me tonight.

So, I go for diversion before she digs up that bone.

"Why'd you only grab one?"

That vee between her eyes deepens and she tilts her head to the side, studying me. "What?"

"That's a big ass cupcake, tiny tornado, and it's the middle of the night." I move over to her, snag a knife and a second fork, tapping her lightly on the shoulder with the fork before I open the cabinet above her head and grab out two plates. "So we're going to share."

There's a long pause.

Long enough for me to pull out the candles, set them in the top of the plastic container, and start slicing the giant cupcake in half.

Should I be eating this in the middle of the night when I have a game tomorrow—*er*—today?

Nope. Definitely not.

Does it look too good to pass up?

Definitely yes.

And, fuck it.

It's my birthday.

I'm eating a fucking cupcake.

"We're going to share?"

Her tone is so strange, so *not* the Luna I remember that I glance over at her, trying to ferret out why it sounds wrong.

But the moment my eyes hit hers she glances away and I lose out on any hope of that.

Hmm.

"Yeah, Luns," I say. "We're going to share."

She looks back, and it's like a different woman's appeared—light and bright has returned, and her smile is wide, glazed over and confident, but *fake*. "Well," she says lightly, "if you're sharing, I get the bigger half."

I snort, know the moment's passed.

If she doesn't want to explain, she'll keep that shit locked down.

And it's late.

I have hockey tomorrow—today. I don't have time for decades old contracts or arguing about sharing a cupcake or reorganizing my kitchen or figuring out how in the fuck Luna found me now, after all this time.

So instead of arguing, I just keep slicing, peeling back the paper and lifting one half—the bigger half—onto one of the plates. "Eat, tiny tornado," I order softly, holding it up.

Gray eyes on mine.

Holding. Searching.

I know mine are likely as unfathomable as hers were moments ago.

But I don't lower the plate.

And I know when she realizes that I'm not playing around either, that my stubborn streak has come out, that I'm not eating this alone.

Do I know why I haven't addressed the whole *getting married* thing? Nope.

Or maybe it's another yes, but I don't *want* to address it situation.

Either way, she takes the plate.

I serve up the other half, plunk it onto the plate, and break off a chunk with my fork, shoving it into my mouth.

And promptly moaning.

God, what's it about store-bought cake with heaps of buttercream that tastes so damned good?

Nostalgia, I guess.

I open my eyes, scoop up another bite, and shove it into my mouth. Then freeze when I see she's watching me.

Closely.

Intently.

"What?" I ask through my bite.

She tilts her head to the side again and my heart pulses. Cute. She was always cute. And tempting. And...left me obsessed.

Wanting.

But I'm not a teenager now.

I'm a grown man. I'm in control of my emotions, my feelings, my *obsessions*.

Except apparently, when she moves toward me, setting her plate beside mine, lifting a hand and placing the palm lightly on my chest.

My heart beats faster.

My dick twitches.

My brain conveniently forgets about the whole marriage contract thing.

Especially when she murmurs, "You haven't changed at all, have you?"

FOUR

Luna

I DIDN'T MEAN to come this close, didn't mean to touch him, to say that.

But I couldn't have predicted the effect my words have on him.

His hand settles on my hip, drawing me steadily closer to the hard planes of his body. "I think I've changed a lot, tiny tornado." A pause, long and drawn out, same as his eyes tracing down my body. "We both have." Another tug has me flush against him.

And I feel the change.

A *big* one.

And yeah, I said *he* hadn't changed, but I just meant on the inside.

Because the outside of Aiden is markedly different, and the way I'm suddenly pressed flush to him feeling all that I'm feeling is different in the best possible way. So much more intense than teenage infatuation, than a few kisses snuck here and there.

The inside, though.

That's familiar.

That's *Aiden*.

Safe and good and always something I can rely on.

My home when the realities of living with my family were...well, what they were.

All of that familiar, all of that safe...it flows through me and I melt against him. "I missed you, Aiden," I murmur. "A lot."

"Is that why you decided to show up on my doorstep and wake me up at two in the morning after all this time?"

Guilt slices through me.

He's still talking though, so I tuck it away, stow it to flagellate myself later.

"Is that why you still have it?" he asks.

"It?" I hedge, even though I know exactly what he's talking about.

The marriage contract.

The whole reason I knocked on his door at two in the morning.

"Luns," he murmurs, settling his hands on my shoulders and leaning back. Holding my gaze, lifting a brow, and...

I give.

Just a little.

"I moved back home."

Surprise sliding through his green eyes. "*You* moved home?"

A pulse of pain, my throat going tight. "Grams died eight months ago," I push out, and the truth of saying that aloud is so agonizing that I can barely stay standing, barely fathom surviving it.

She was...

The only bright spot.

Except for Aiden.

"Oh, sweetheart," he murmurs.

And then I'm held tightly against him again, wrapped up in that safe and familiar. He smooths one hand up and down my spine.

"You should have come sooner," he orders.

"I didn't know you were back in California," I whisper. "I just happened to see you pop up on the TV." I push lightly at his chest, gaining enough distance for me to see his face again, to stare into green eyes I once knew better than my own. "You made it," I tell him, touching his jaw, smiling up at him, the pride I have for him and all his hard work cutting through the grief, the worry, the strain that have eaten me up ever since I got the call that Grams was sick a year ago.

"I did," he murmurs.

"I am *so* proud of you."

A blip of quiet, his arms tightening slightly, and I don't miss the slight flush that appears on his cheeks, the hint of red that is just as adorable now as it was when we were teenagers. "Thanks, Luns," he says softly, and then—of course he does—he changes the subject from himself.

Humble.

Sweet.

But a boy destined for much greater things than me.

Then, *Luns*, why the fuck are you here with that stupid contract that means nothing in hand—at two o'clock in the morning—on his damned birthday?

Desperation.

But my desperation isn't so great as to fuck up Aiden's life.

This was crazy, coming here at all.

I knew that, but...

This is *Aiden*.

No. I'm not going to do this, not with him, not ever.

"Finish your cupcake," I tell him, carefully extracting myself from his hold, going back to mine. He lets me go, and I hate the blips of hurt, of longing, of despair ricocheting through my middle that turn my insides to ribbons as I move away.

This is pretty much the best way this all could have gone—he didn't kick me out, didn't call the police, didn't...

Have a woman in his bed demanding to know who the hell I am.

Right. Yeah.

That would have been worse.

"How did it happen?" he asks between bites.

How did I get here with my life in shambles, barely making it paycheck to paycheck, the one thing I cared about from my fucked up childhood about to be shredded to pieces?

The Maybelle family curse.

Or the one that seems to strike only the female members of my family.

My mom. My sister. Grams. *Me.*

"Luns?"

I jerk, gaze colliding with his. "Yeah?"

"If you don't want to talk about Grams then we don't have to."

Damn.

Why does he still have to be so nice?

"It's not that," I admit on a sigh.

"Then what?"

"I just can't believe that she's gone. That they're all gone—my mom, my sister, Grams. I—" My voice breaks and even though it's not the impetus that brought me here, that had me spending every free moment of the last week of my life on the internet, searching for Aiden, for where he might live, until I finally found his address and knew that if I waited for the light of day, reason would take over and I would shove the stupid marriage contract back in the box of my childhood memories and just deal with what lay ahead alone.

Alone.

God, I hate that word.

That reality.

"I woke up the morning after she was gone," I push out, "and realized I have no one. My brother. My dad. They're..." I trail off, eyes stinging.

He waits as my thoughts spin and my words find a way back.

"They haven't changed," I finish. "And I found the contract when I was packing my stuff up to take over to Gram's place, and then I saw you on TV"—both of those statements are true —"and it seemed like the universe was guiding me toward you, bringing you back to me." Also true. So true that my throat stoppers up for a long moment and my next words are raspy. "Because you were the one person left who wasn't like *them.*"

He's silent for a long moment.

Then he sets his fork on the plate, crosses back over to me.

And I get Aiden again—safe and warm, gentle and kind.

"You know what I was thinking?" he murmurs, voice soft, arms tight. "Before I fell asleep last night?"

I shake my head.

"I was thinking about how alone I am. My parents are doing their retirement thing. My siblings are all busy with their families and jobs and lives that don't revolve around my shitty hockey schedule."

My heart squeezes.

"And they're not going to be here on my birthday," he murmurs.

He shrugs.

But I don't miss the note of hurt in his words.

"I'm a grownup. I don't need my family here on my birthday. I know they have lives and jobs and vacations and kids and retirement. I just…" Another shrug. "They'll call," he says. "I know they will and they'll mean the Happy Birthdays they wish me. But I won't be with them and I'm not with the Breakers anymore so I don't have them either. And the Grizzles are fine but I don't know where I'm fitting in with them yet, don't know my place, not really…" He shakes his head. "Sorry," he says. "I'm rambling and taking over. I just wanted to say that I know a little of what it likes to feel lonely, so I'm glad—however it came to be—that you're here now and neither of us are alone."

He's still so sweet.

Big and strong and bearded but with a gentle, beautiful soul that feels deeply.

It's why I fell in love with him as a teenager.

And why I ultimately let him go.

And it's why I fall a little for him right now.

And maybe it's why—or maybe it's just that he's big and strong and bearded *and* pressed against me—that I do what I do next.

I flatten my palm over his heart, feel the steady beat below.

"Maybe we don't have to be alone," I say as I lift on tiptoe.

His hands tighten on my hips. "Luns?"

"Maybe we can be *us* again."

And then…

I slant my mouth over his.

FIVE

Aiden

IT ONLY TAKES a heartbeat for me to realize this kiss isn't like the stolen ones from our teenage years, sloppy smooches that we hurried through or sneaked in, hiding in the shadows of the parking lot, waiting for our parents to come pick us up.

This is...

Well, I'm not thinking about being alone—not at fucking *all* —that's for damn sure.

I dive my hand into her hair, tilting her head back, deepening the kiss in a way I never could have imagined all those years before.

Lips parting. Sleek darts of our tongues as they battle for dominance. Moans vibrating up her throat, dancing down mine. It takes all of ten seconds and I'm hard, harder than I've ever been before—even as a teenager, sneaking those kisses.

She's...Luna.

But the Luna I never could have imagined—curvy and

beautiful, smelling amazing, like flowers and woman, and tasting like cupcakes.

I need more.

I need *her*.

Bending, I scoop her up, setting her on the edge of the counter, taking advantage of the height so I don't have to bend down quite so far to kiss her.

She moans again and her arms wind around my neck, body arching against mine, kissing me back with an abandon that threatens to burn its way through my control.

And the flames intensify when she wraps her legs around me, grinds against the ride of my erection.

"Fuck," I groan into her mouth, rocking right back against her, wishing I could make the layers of clothes disappear with one thought flashing through my mind.

When that doesn't work, I reach for the hem of her shirt.

Then my conscience smacks me upside the head.

I manage to snag the frayed edges before they can fully snap and fly free, pausing for long enough to pull back, to study her face again, both of us breathing heavy. "Luns," I say softly, cupping her jaw. "We don't have to do this. You can crash in my guest room and if you're not tired we can watch infomercials on TV until we pass out."

Yes, my dick is threatening to explode.

But this is a lot—her showing up out of the blue in the middle of the night—and I know she's still grieving Grams, same as I know that this woman is different too. The same...yet changed.

And because...I wanted her when I was a teenager.

So much that I dreamed of more than kissing—and that I did it for years.

But she was the one to firmly stop us from going there.

Same as she was the one who distanced herself when I left to play juniors.

Doing this now, with all of the pieces of the past and present tangling...well, it doesn't feel right.

Something passes across her face, something I can't read because it's there and gone so quickly. Before I can ask her to explain, her hands land on my shoulders, nails kneading lightly at my flesh, and I get the distinct notion that she's trying to distract me when she asks, "Haven't you thought about it?"

I can't lie to her.

"Yes," I rasp out. Far too many times and for far too long.

"I used to dream about it," she murmurs, nails digging in a little harder. "Used to think about those stolen kisses turning into more, used to hope that you'd sneak in through my bedroom window at night, crawl into bed beside me, pull the blankets back, and—"

My dick goes even harder.

This woman is going to be the death of me.

"Luns—"

"I imagined you touching me," she whispers, nails digging in a little deeper, the slight bite of pain further eroding my control. "Kissing me just like this. Making me feel good." Her mouth kicks up. "Though, I think you may have a few more skills at making me feel good now."

I do.

My mind is fucking spinning with all the ways to help her fall apart on my lips and tongue, my fingers, my cock. Still—

"You're grieving, tiny tornado," I tell her gently. "And you don't need to bring a contract or kiss me"—or *more*—"to stay here, to talk about her, to be friends again."

She jerks.

Then her eyes slam closed.

But not before I see the tears.

"Christ, Luns," I whisper, tugging her off the counter and up into my arms. She turns her head away, body going stiff.

Her efforts at controlling her emotions come too late.

The first drops of her tears escape the cage of her eyelashes, sliding down her cheeks, dripping off her jaw and plunking onto my shirt.

Then her chest hitches, a sob escaping, so forlorn that my heart squeezes roughly.

"I-I sh-shouldn't have come here," she whispers. "Sh-shouldn't have brought that stupid contract. And I-I shouldn't st-still be here. You have a life, have a family. You don't need my bullshit fucking it up a-and—" Her words devolve into sobs.

I carry her over to the couch, settle onto the cushions with her in my lap.

And then I hold her.

Until, long minutes later, her sobs subside and her body relaxes against mine, and she murmurs, voice raspy from her crying, "I'm such a mess."

"A beautiful mess," I say softly, wiping at the tear tracks streaked across her cheeks.

She laughs, but it's watery, and shakes her head. "Only Aiden Black would be this nice when a psycho from his past shows up, waving a contract that only a teenager would agree to, and then hold said psycho while she cries her eyes out."

I leave the contract thing alone for the moment.

There's more there.

Things that don't make sense—it's more than a preamble to bring us together again, more than an excuse that brought her to my door.

But that'll hold.

Right now, she's hurting.

"You miss her," I murmur, tucking her hair behind her ear. "Grams," I add, probably unnecessarily.

A shaky breath, her lids sliding closed again, hiding those storm cloud gray eyes from me once more. I hate that, want to demand she open them, that she'll let me stare into the depths until they give up all her secrets.

But that's not Luna.

She is—*was*—complicated, the Shrek equivalent of that onion, those secrets revealed layer by layer by *layer*.

"I do miss her," she whispers. "A lot."

And I hear more there too—pain and grief and a slender thread of anger.

But today I need to alleviate her pain, take some of the weight of that grief away.

"I remember when Grams came to that Winter Open, when you first started competing. Do you?"

She opens her eyes, and I can't lie that pride ripples through me when I see the amusement in those stormy gray depths. "I remember," she says, lips turning up. "Mostly because I swore that after she yelled at the judges like that I would never—*ever*—compete again."

I chuckle. "She didn't lose her temper often, but when she did…"

"Kaboom," Luna finishes.

"Exactly." I draw her a little closer. "And she was right to yell at them. They totally fucked you over with that low ball of a score."

"I fell on my axel!"

"One of the other girls fell twice," I remind her. "And the last one skated off the ice crying halfway through because she realized people were watching her."

I get her then.

The Luna of old instead of the sad Luna I'm holding who's full of grief and shadows and pain.

She laughs and it's not soft. It's loud and full-bodied and…

Fuck, but how can I still want her now—after all this time, after spending, what?, thirty minutes with her—just as much as I wanted her back then when she forced me to let her go.

But I do.

And it's not just because she's beautiful.

It's because she's *Luna*.

"Now," I say, shoving that thought away to deal with later and setting her beside me on the couch. "I'm going to grab our plates, we'll to eat our cupcake to celebrate our birthdays, and then we're going to find somewhere to stream *Wheel of Fortune* so we can give Grams a proper send-off, okay?"

She's quiet as I stand up, as I cross into the kitchen and snag the plates.

But as I'm walking back, she whispers, "It's supposed to be *your* birthday."

"What's that, tiny tornado?" I ask, distracted by the sight of her sitting on my couch...and how right it feels to have her there.

"It's supposed to be your birthday, so why are you the one who's giving me a gift?"

"First, it's *our* birthday." I touch her cheek. "And second, who's to say you're not giving me one right back?"

SIX

Luna

LAST THING I remember is thinking that R, S, T, L, N, and E aren't all that helpful when my brain is inching toward sleep.

Now, I feel rested.

Pleasantly warm and my head is cushioned on something that's not strictly soft, but also isn't so hard that it's left me rising to consciousness with a crick in my neck.

Instead, I woke up because...I'm refreshed?

Which is strange.

I can't remember the last time I connected more than three or four hours in a row.

At first, it was because Grams needed something in the middle of the night—medication or help to the bathroom. Then it was because I was worried she wasn't waking me up, that something had happened, even though the night nurse was caring for her.

Then it was because I worried if I slept I would wake up and she'd be gone and—

I'd have missed it.

My last chance at telling her I love her, at holding her hand, at being by her side.

And after...was the funeral, the burial, clearing out her room and...reading the will.

Realizing that she could still affect my life, even from the other side.

Now, as I open my eyes, I realize why I'm comfortable, why I slept more than those aforementioned three or four hours.

I'm not at home—not at Gram's place, not even at the family home where my brother and dad live, boundaries trodden on, privacy not respected, and sleeping hours certainly not abided by.

When I lived with them there was always a coffee grinder going or cabinets being slammed or knocks on my door because they need something from me.

So, Gram's place was the natural conclusion. Plus, it was the only house that ever felt like home anyway. It's just...it hasn't been easy to hold on to for a girl making twenty dollars an hour.

Neither is paying the crippling lawyer fees, especially when I'm cut off from the family coffers.

Thus, my father and brother's war on wearing me down, on getting me to give in has continued.

And I'm stuck.

But...for once I'm not in my own bed, dealing with their bullshit.

I'm rested and—

A soft snore.

I'm with *Aiden*.

In his arms. In his—

I finally process what I'm seeing.

Aiden's bedroom.

Navy walls, gray curtains on the windows, mahogany furniture. A mirror on the far wall, a—I shift slightly, trying to see, my lips curving when I do. The man has an area rug, thick and plush and patterned.

With swirls of blue and gray.

There's art on the walls—a cityscape that gives tribute to Baltimore, where he played for the Breakers, and also one of this coast, depicting the craggy cliffs that surround the Pacific, worn into complex patterns over thousands and thousands of years of wind and rain and waves.

A rug. Art. Curtains. Matching furniture.

He really *is* all grown up.

"What are you smiling about?"

I jerk then shift again, this time in the circle of Aiden's arms, finding his eyes open, the emerald depths sparkling with curiosity. He lifts a hand, traces lightly along the curve of my mouth, and I'm a little surprised to find that I *am* smiling.

"You have a rug."

His brow lifts.

"And matching curtains and a furniture set and"—I tug lightly at the covers—"an actual bedspread and corresponding sheets."

Now *his* mouth curves. "And that's worth smiling about?"

"You're all grown up, Aiden Black."

"Sheets and a rug?" He laughs. "That's all it takes?"

"Yup." I shrug as well as I'm able. "Or, well, those and the curtains and the matching furniture and the artwork."

He chuckles, shakes his head, lightly tapping the tip of my nose. "What about your bedroom? What color are the sheets?"

I don't mean to. It just...slips out. "Why?" I tease. "So you can imagine me naked in them later?"

His eyes go molten, burning into mine. "No, sweetheart,"

he murmurs, sliding one big, warm hand along my side. "If I'm going to imagine you anywhere, it's beneath me in *my* bed."

"But you..." My brow furrows even as my body inches closer to his, seeking out the heat and strength of him.

"I what?" he presses.

I nibble my lip but don't bother prevaricating. This is Aiden. *My* Aiden. "You stopped us last night."

His expression gentles, that hand stills, resting on my hip, thumb tracing back and forth, back and forth. "I don't think you were in the right frame of mind, do you?"

He's right.

I was...

Well, not in the *right frame of mind* is pretty much the nicest thing that someone could say about the tangle of desperation and need, desire and fondness and attraction for the man I'm currently sprawled half on top of.

"And that adorable wrinkle of your nose tells me that I'm right but you don't want to admit it."

My nose wrinkles further.

He chuckles. Then taps the tip of it. "So... that marriage contract."

I tense.

Which is precisely the wrong thing to do.

It tells him his fishing expedition is right.

And I'm not ready to talk about it—don't have a good excuse to make him forget all about it before I take myself and my problems back out of his life.

So, I enact evasive maneuvers.

"Aiden?" I ask softly.

"Yeah, Luns?"

God, I love that he still hardly ever calls me my real name—it's always Luns or sweetheart or tiny tornado (though I'm not so tiny any longer).

Focus.

"So was the whole stopping the kiss thing last night because you were being a gentleman?" I ask, settling my hand on his chest, feeling the muscles there tighten. "Or," I whisper, "was it because I was doing something you *didn't* want?"

His hand on my hip tightens and then he draws me a little closer.

Close enough for me to feel the hard length of his erection.

"Does *that* feel like you were doing something I don't want?"

I shrug as well as I'm able to in this position. "That proves nothing."

One second, he's beneath me.

The next, he's rolled up, pinning me into the mattress, hot green eyes on mine. "No?" he asks, parting my thighs and sinking more heavily onto me.

"Nope," I say, popping the p. My mouth twitches, even though I try to affect seriousness.

"No?" His eyes dance.

"Nope," I repeat. "That's just morning wood."

"Morning—" His mouth drops open and he freezes, gaping at me. Then he does the most wonderful thing.

He tosses his head back and laughs.

SEVEN

Aiden

I LAUGH and she joins in.

Fuck she's funny.

And beautiful.

And below me.

And the vibration of our laughter feels really, *really* good.

Something that has me freezing.

"Luns?" I ask.

She stops giggling, as though suddenly realizing our positions. "Yeah?" she whispers.

I lean in, drop my voice to a whisper too. "I can't remember there being a time where I didn't want you."

Her lungs inflate in a rush, shock flickering across her face.

Bending, I take advantage of surprising her, pressing my mouth to hers, slipping my tongue between her parted lips, tasting her and doing it long and slow and deep.

She hooks a leg around my waist and the change in position...it's glorious.

Our pelvises align and I can feel the heat of her through the thin material of her sweats.

Christ, I need her...almost as much as I need the layers of fabric currently between us to disappear like a puff of smoke.

Unable to stop myself, I rock against her, loving that the motion has her wrapping her other leg around me, has her grinding against the ridge of my erection, our bodies comfortable together, remembering each other, moving instinctively toward something that will bring pleasure to both of us.

Even though we've never moved like this together before.

Even though we've never been here—horizontal in a bed—before.

Yes, we have history—innocent kisses and gentle caresses, teenage bodies pressed close in shadowy corners, hesitant touches of soft curves.

But there's no hesitation now.

Not from me.

Not from her.

I slide my hand along her side, dragging the material of her shirt up along with it, exposing delicate skin and curves I need to get my mouth on.

I lean back onto my heels, tugging her up with me.

"What are you—"

But I don't let her finish the question, just drag the material over her head and toss it to the side.

"Christ," I mutter. "Where'd you get those, Luns?"

Her mouth quirks, but she's breathing as heavily as I am—something that's great viewing as far as I'm concerned, those plump mounds nearly toppling out of the lacy edge of her bra with each rapid inhalation and exhalation. "I kind of grew up," she says. "Something that seems to be catching, big shot." A hand drifting down my front, then stopping, fingertips tapping *oh so close* to the tip of my cock.

I chuckle softly, take one more second to soak in the gorgeous view of Luna.

Then I reach a hand around behind her, undoing the clasps of her bra.

We both groan when her tits are freed, then I do again when I yank the material down her arms, toss it in the direction of her shirt.

God, her breasts are glorious, bouncing slightly, the pink tips hard and demanding that I suck.

"Hey—!"

A slightly outraged cry because I've pushed her shoulders, sending her toppling to her back, those tits bouncing all over again.

But it doesn't last long.

Instead, her outrage turns into a cry of pleasure as I bend and take one hard bud into my mouth, suckling deeply, loving the sound of her calling out my name, loving how her moans fill the air, how her body arches beneath mine.

I cup her breast, positioning it so I can pay proper homage to that beautiful nipple, then massage her other tit, rolling her nipple between thumb and forefinger.

"Aiden!" she cries, but I don't stop, just kiss my way over to her other side, tasting and sucking, licking and nibbling. The scent of her, the feel of her, the *sound* of her—it's intoxicating. "I need—" Her head thrashes on the pillow, hips bucking against mine, and as much as I want to stay right where I am, we both need more.

Releasing her breast, I move down, kissing my way over her torso, making my way to the waistband of her sweats and shoving the bedspread off in the process.

I drag them down, whip them off her legs, tossing them in the direction of her shirt and bra.

"This is underwear?" I ask softly, tracing my finger over the lacy scrap of fabric that's masquerading as panties.

"You like them," she pants. "So...mission accomplished."

Grinning, I draw them along lush thighs, down shapely calves, off feet with pink-painted toenails.

Then I place one hand on each of her legs and push them wide.

"Fuck," I growl at the sight of all that slick, plump pink.

Her pelvis tilts, hips arching, silently begging for my mouth.

So, I give it to her—trailing my tongue through her folds, arrowing in on her clit, discovering with just a few short strokes exactly what she likes.

And then repeating that while I discover *other* things she likes.

A finger pressing deep, curling up, matching the slow licks. Another joining in, fucking her steadily in time to the flick of my tongue. The flat of my tongue circling her clit. A nip to soft, wet flesh—

"Aiden!" she shouts, entire body bucking.

Okay then.

She likes teeth.

Grinning, I redouble my efforts, lick and fuck, stroke and bite, and it doesn't take long before her pussy convulses around my fingers, her hips grind faster against my mouth, her moans grow louder and more frequently until...

Her pussy grows even slicker.

Her body goes taut.

And...she comes apart.

"Oh, my God!" she cries, neck arched, eyes closed, legs tight around my shoulders, that wet cunt of hers spasming around my fingers. "Oh, my fucking *God*."

I coax her down gently even though my cock is about to break in half. Because I want this to be good for her, want this to be the best fucking ever.

Because as the day goes on, I want her to remember it was me who brought her pleasure, me who made her feel good.

I want her to remember *me*.

To let me back in.

All the way in.

Speaking of which...

"Aiden," she moans softly, eyes slitting open, those gray irises hazy and drunk on pleasure. "I need you." She reaches for me, tugging at my shoulders. "I need you inside me."

Yes.

Fuck, yes.

I need that too.

I stretch for my nightstand, tug open the drawer, searching for a condom, thinking about how I'm going to finally get to thrust into the tight, slick heat when...

I hear it.

No. Fuck no.

I freeze, fingers wrapped around the plastic-covered square.

"What?" Luna asks, eyes half mast, legs spreading an inch wider.

Showing me all that I could have—

If only things were different.

Because then I hear it again. The scrape of metal against metal.

With growing horror, I swivel my head toward the open door of my bedroom.

More noises.

The sound of a key in a lock. The squeak of the condo's door being pushed open.

Then a voice.

My *mother's* voice echoing down the hall.

"Happy Birthday, honey!"

EIGHT

Luna

THE WORDS TAKE a second to penetrate...mostly because Aiden *isn't* doing any penetrating of his own.

Even though I'm desperate for it. Even though I asked for it.

Even though I can feel him practically vibrating with need as he reaches for a condom.

Even though I'm shaking from my orgasm, my body still humming with aftershocks of pleasure...and the need for more.

For *him*.

So yeah, it takes a minute for the voice, the words, the *footsteps* to penetrate.

Aiden reacts faster, jumping off me, grabbing the blankets from the floor and tossing them over me...

Right as the footsteps grow louder, loud enough that I process exactly how close they are—that being directly outside Aiden's bedroom.

And his door is open.

"Fuck," I whisper, earning a flash of emerald eyes, one blazing second of contact that sears my insides, sends my pulse skyrocketing, my heart thudding hard against my rib cage.

That quick glance reveals nothing except that he's feeling something big.

And I don't know if it's regret.

Or worry that I'm naked and people are walking toward us.

Or that it's a woman calling out Happy Birthday.

The last is the worst. Or maybe the first—because if he regrets what we just did...I close my eyelids for a heartbeat, exhale silently.

The only one that doesn't make me want to curl up into a tiny ball and pretend that the last eight hours—hell, the last eight days, eight months—haven't actually happened is the middle one.

But it also doesn't feel great.

Because I made a promise to myself last night that I wasn't going through with this, wasn't going to dump my shit on his doorstep...

And I'm still here.

I don't have time to sit in those emotions, those regrets, because the footsteps come to a crescendo and Aiden is hurrying toward that open doorway.

He doesn't make it there first.

A woman steps into the open doorway, and that has me clinging to the comforter Aiden tossed over me, wanting to melt into the sheets, the mattress, hoping for the floor to magically swallow me up and deposit me onto the street below.

Preferably with my clothes on.

But I'd take any escape at this point.

A man follows the woman. And then another woman, this one younger, and two more men follow her, both around the younger woman's age.

No, I think.

I *realize*—my horror growing.

Because I know that the younger woman is thirty-two, her brothers—including Aiden—twenty-nine, twenty-seven, and... today, or rather at two-something last night, twenty-*five*.

Aiden's family is standing in his hallway.

Shit.

This can't be happening.

Not when I'm naked and in his bed and—

"Surprise, baby!" his mother, Kathy, cries, rushing forward, closing the last bit of difference between them and throwing her arms around Aiden's neck. "You didn't honestly think that we would let your birthday pass without us being here, did you?"

"We even bought tickets to tonight's game!" Matt, his dad, says, swooping in when Kathy releases him, giving Aiden one of those man hugs with not a ton of arm wrapping but lots of back slapping.

But then my mind locks on to something else.

Because...*shit.*

He has a game tonight?

And I showed up out of the blue at two in the morning? Then kept him up for hours?

I'm a dick.

A big, giant dick with dicky selfish tendencies and horrible timing and—

I'm...well, I'm a dick.

Something I must verbalize because I draw Carrie, Aiden's sister's, focus. "Um, Mom?" she stage whispers, eyes going wide. "Maybe we should head back into the, um,...."

Kathy is too busy smiling at Aiden and looping her arm through Matt's, resting her head on his shoulder to listen to her daughter. "We surprised you, didn't we?"

Carrie nudges Ralph and I watch Aiden's brother's eyes flare with surprise as they drift over to me on the bed, where I'm still doing my best to disappear into the blankets.

Shit. *Shit.*

Why is this happening?

And *why*, I realize, when I manage to tear my eyes from Carrie and Ralph does my underwear and bra have to be all of two feet inside the room.

Front and center in front of the open door where Aiden's family have gathered.

Something Ralph notices, apparently, his gaze going to the pile of my clothes, his brows shooting up, his elbow jerking out to jab at Aiden's other brother, Dave's, side.

"Stop," he hisses, smacking Ralph away.

"Mom. Dad," Aiden says, reaching for the door. "Let's go to the front room and—"

"Ow!" Dave glares at Ralph for a second but another rough prod of his brother's elbow shuts him up...and clues him into my position in the bed.

Wide green eyes locked onto mine.

Then returning to his siblings. "Um, Mom," Dave begins. "We really should go out into the living room—" A tilt of his head back down the hall.

"Not until I've gotten my fill of my baby boy." Kathy leans in and hugs him again. "I'm just so happy to see you. Twenty-five." A sniff, her fingers dashing beneath each eye before she hugs him again. "My baby is all grown up now. So strong and tall and—"

Her eyes drift over his shoulder.

Come to a rest on mine.

Flare with shock, her mouth falling open.

Fuck my life.

"Oh, my God." She drops back down onto her heels,

leaning around Aiden and hissing at Matt. "My baby has a girlfriend?" She turns her glare to Aiden. "*You* have a girlfriend and you haven't told me?"

Seriously. Fuck. My. Life.

This can't be happening.

"Right," Carrie says, taking charge and, thankfully, finally putting me out of my misery. She reaches for her mother. "We've done the surprise part. Now we need to go back out to the living room and wait for them to—"

Kathy swats at Aiden's chest. "You have a girlfriend and her underwear is on the floor and we haven't even met her yet!"

I bite back a groan, clutch the blankets even more tightly to my chest, know that my cheeks have gone fire engine red.

Please, universe. Please just help me disappear.

Just this once.

"Mom," Aiden says, bending and—thank fuck—scooping up my bra and underwear, stuffing them into the pocket of his sweats. "Look. There's a lot happening right now—"

That's the understatement of the fucking year, isn't it?

"—but I need you to take a breath and walk back out to the living room. Make yourself a cup of coffee. Hell, have a beer if you need one to chill the fuck out—"

"Aiden," Matt says quietly. "Language."

"I will watch my language," Aiden replies, just as quietly, but with a lot more deadly intent and something inside me softens at the protective note in his voice, unfurling dangerously, "when you get the fuck out of my bedroom and away from my fucking woman."

The air goes taut.

Matt's chest puffs up.

Kathy's gasps.

Thankfully Carrie and the others have my—or their brother's, I suppose—back.

Carrie steps forward, snags her mother's arm, drawing Kathy out of the open doorway and in the direction of the living room.

Ralph and Dave position themselves on opposite sides of Matt. "Come on, Dad," Ralph mutters. "Let's wait out front for Aiden, okay?"

Matt's eyes narrow but then they slide to me, still frozen and under blankets, the material clutched tightly beneath my chin.

"Dad," Dave presses.

He turns away, but maybe his expression softens as he starts to rotate, maybe there's a hint of sympathy beneath that tough, hockey dad exterior.

Maybe.

Because the next moment, he's gone, ushered out by Ralph and Dave.

Leaving Aiden and me alone.

"A girlfriend!" I hear echo down the hall. "How can he have a girlfriend and I don't even know her!"

Fuck.

We're alone, yes.

And yet, still without a lick of privacy.

NINE

Aiden

I CLOSE the door on my mom's surprised accusations—something I know is the direct result of me denying that I'm dating anyone...

Precisely two days ago.

The thing is...I wasn't.

I'm *not*.

I just have a naked woman in my bed, her underwear and bra in my pocket...and a marriage contract on my kitchen counter.

With my mother in arm's reach.

Fuck.

But...bigger problems first.

"Are you okay?" I ask Luns softly, hurrying across the room, sitting on the edge of the mattress. "I..." I sigh. "I know that was a lot."

She snorts, lifts a shaky hand to her forehead, pushing back her hair. "A lot is your family showing up out of the blue for dinner when the only thing I know how to cook is broccoli stew."

"Broccoli stew?" I say, humor coiling in my belly.

"Shut up you," she mutters. *"That"*—a jerk of her head toward the closed door—"was a lot if you call a freaking nuclear bomb a tiny little explosion. *That* was a lot if you think a Category Five hurricane is just a bit of rain. *That*—"

"Luns."

"—was a lot if you think that Pedro Pascal is just another actor."

Christ, she's funny.

But I think if I start laughing right now she'll pick up my lamp and brain me with it.

The Pedro thing, though, *that* I'm storing away in my mind to bring back up later.

It's gotta be the biceps.

Why did extra arm exercises suddenly get scratched onto my workouts?

"That—"

I lean down and slant my lips over hers, kissing her until she relaxes, until she sighs softly into my mouth. "I'll fix this," I tell her as I pull back, cupping her jaw lightly. "You just get dressed."

A scowl. A wrinkle of that adorable nose.

"Thank you for reminding me that I was naked in front of your entire family."

"Technically you were under the blankets."

"*Naked* under the blankets."

I tap her nose. "Which is another why you should get dressed."

Her mouth falls open then clamps together, eyes flashing with irritation, the little sparks of lightning in the gray depths threatening to strike at me. "You—"

But I just steal another kiss then push up to my feet, pull her bra and underwear out of my pocket and toss them at her. Then I snag her sweats and shirt from the floor, drop them beside her.

"Me," I agree. "I'm a pain in the ass."

She scowls then mutters begrudgingly. "At least you're a pain in the ass who gives great orgasms."

My dick twitches and I shake my head at her. "Behave."

Finally, she smiles. "Never."

I chuckle, start for the door.

"Get dressed, tiny tornado, and I'll handle my family."

"TRY THIS, SWEETHEART!" my mom declares, shoving the apple turnover in Luna's direction.

Luna, who's spent the last hour being practically force-fed pastries at Molly's, widens her eyes at me.

"Mom," I begin.

But just like back in my condo, where walking out into the living room intent on handling the craziness that is my family... I'm completely ignored, any plans of getting them to disappear so Luna and I could finish celebrating our birthdays totally derailed.

"Try it," my mom demands, waving it at her again.

"Thank you, Kathy," Luns says politely, "but really, I'm full."

"Pish," my mom says, shaking her head. "Full only counts with airplanes and trash cans."

I frown, trying to make sense of the nonsense my mom is spouting—and deciding she's not wrong—but before I can get back to rescue Luns from carb overload, Carrie reaches in, snagging the apple turnover and beginning the extremely hard work of disposing of it in her stomach.

Speaking of trash cans.

Heh.

"Mom," she says between bites, so really, it comes out as *Shmwom.* "Cool it on force-feeding Luna food. You've already put her through the wringer enough."

"But this is *Luna*," my mom says. "*Our* Luna."

Right.

Something else that didn't go as planned.

Because they remembered Luna about two seconds after I mentioned her name. Which meant that by the time Luns made her way out of my bedroom—fully dressed, thankfully (or maybe not for me, considering exactly what my family interrupted)—they remembered everything: Luna my best friend from the rink; Luna the girl I had a crush on; Luna the girl from the troubled family.

No mom. Workaholic dad. Brother who was—and presumably still is—a total dick.

And now the one solid in her life, Grams, gone.

It took exactly thirty seconds after *that* summary for my mom to declare that Luna was joining us for my birthday breakfast at Molly's—and that it had just become *our* birthday breakfast.

Mostly so Luns wouldn't be alone on her birthday.

And also because she needs to *put some meat* on her bones.

Hence the force-feeding.

The only positive is that my mom fussing over Luna meant that I was able to secure the marriage contract.

Not that it's a real contract.

Not that it really means anything.

So why then had I carefully tucked it into a drawer in my

office, treating the paper like it's more fragile that the Declaration Of Independence?

A good question.

But another one for later.

Because my mom has picked up another pastry.

God help us.

I swear, I didn't mind the solo celebration becoming a joint one, especially since it meant more time with Luns and she never minded hanging with my family before. But this isn't helping me endear myself to my tiny tornado, isn't helping her stay so I can get to the truth of what's bothering her, isn't helping me keep her close enough for us to figure out who and what *us* is.

"Mom," I say, allowing a bit of sharp into my tone. "Enough with the pastries. We've all eaten our body weight of muffins and turnovers. Consider our birthdays celebrated. Now, I want to hear about you guys."

My dad, who spends most of his existence zoning out and seemingly dissociating from my mom's chattering, slants me a warning look.

Telling me to be careful.

To not take it too far with my mom. To be respectful and considerate.

I'm reading all that loud and clear.

But I'm also not going to allow my mom to run roughshod over Luna—or to continue doing so, anyway.

I love my mom.

But she's a handful and a half.

A sliver of amusement slides through me.

Because...kind of like someone else I know.

Someone who's been on their very best behavior as my mom forces her to devour carb after carb.

Thankfully, my dad doesn't get on me like a teenager with

an attitude problem, just takes my mom's hand and the look they exchange has her putting down the next weapon—er, pastry.

"I want to hear about your cruise," I say, taking advantage of my dad's intervention. "And Carrie"—I turn to my sister—"are the girls in town?"

"No," she says. "They have school." A wry smile. "If I'd known about the show, though, I definitely would have brought them." Her eyes flick to mine. "They would have loved it."

My temple throbs.

I'd forgotten.

That Carrie can be a handful too...along with her two preteen daughters.

I shake my head.

"What is it with all the women in my life wanting to torture me?"

"Maybe it's your pretty face," Luna chimes in.

And I smother a groan.

Because I'm surrounded on all sides by troublesome women.

Only...why do I kind of love it?

TEN

Luna

HE'S BEEN VIBRAT NG with energy from the moment I came out of the bedroom.

Something I definitely didn't *want* to do, believe me.

I could have hidden there all day.

But as I slowly dressed, his family didn't show any sign of leaving and anyway, my conscience couldn't handle hiding in the bedroom and leaving Aiden to handle the mess of them finding us indisposed all alone.

So, I made sure all my pertinent parts were covered, fixed my orgasm hair as much as possible, and summoned the courage to make my way out into the front room.

Where I introduced myself.

But that hadn't been necessary—because Kathy remembered me.

"Oh, my God, Luna Maybelle!" Her eyes had lit up. "Evie Maybelle's granddaughter. God, it's been an age since I've seen you!"

And I can't lie that it felt good to be swept into her arms, wrapped tight in a welcoming hug, that Carrie and Ralph, Dave and Matt had all done the same...and that each insisted that I join them at Molly's for a joint birthday breakfast, no matter how much I tried to demure.

Now, we've all gone over to Molly's and I've eaten my body weight in carbs.

I even smoothed things over for Aiden on the whole *girl-friend* front, making an excuse about running into him and reconnecting yesterday—so while his family might think we moved to horizontal fun time too quickly, at least no marriage contracts were mentioned and neither was my internet stalking or middle of the night visit.

But when she finishes telling us about her cruise and focuses back on me, asking a truly dreadful—though, she doesn't know it—question I feel my carefully held together facade begin to crumble., "How is Evie? How is your grandmother?"

God, I miss Grams.

She sees that—or maybe she sees the way Aiden reacts, wrapping an arm around my shoulder and drawing me back against his side, tucking me into his strength.

"Oh honey," she murmurs. "I'm sorry."

But she doesn't go further than that.

Just squeezes my arm and changes the subject to Carrie and the girls—who are about as opposite as two people can get. "And Leslie had three goals last game, but her favorite part was checking the girl on the other team and getting away with it."

Aiden chuckles.

Matt nods approvingly.

"And Simone," Kathy goes on. "Luna, honey, you would not believe what she can play on the piano. It's absolutely beautiful."

"I bet."

Kathy takes my hand. "Now, sweetie pie. I want to hear more about you. Tell me what you've been doing."

Nothing. *Everything.*

Still, I'm not ready to talk about it, Grams and my family, the will and how it's messed with my life, so I keep my explanations carefully vague, not missing the looks Aiden shoots me, telling me he knows precisely what I'm doing.

"And so," I say a tad nervously as I finish up my very glossed over explanation of the last few years, "I get to have Aiden and his gorgeous smile"—I touch his cheek and add, even though I shouldn't because it goes against all those middle of the night promises again—"in my life again."

His face—God, his *eyes.*

They make me both want to run screaming from the bakery...and lean closer to explore all the unsaid things in their deep green depths.

Can't do that.

Shouldn't be here.

And yet...I can't tear myself away.

Can't leave him, leave this family who I already closed myself away from once.

Just...a little more.

I just need a little more time.

"What just went through your mind, sweetheart?" Aiden murmurs, lips brushing along my earlobe as he forms each of the words.

It feels so nice that it takes me a minute to process what he's said.

What I've revealed...and what I further reveal when I go stiff against him.

His brows drag together, eyes flashing with concern. "Luns," he warns.

Thankfully, his family—or rather, his siblings—can't be on their best behavior, not for long anyway.

"Come on, Luns," Ralph teases. "You know it wasn't his smile that got you"—a long trailing look along Aiden's frame—"it's that gorgeous body he works so hard for."

"Shut up," Aiden growls.

"Who are you trying to kid?" Ralph says, ignoring him. "We've all seen your abs, bro. We all know the long hours you pull in the gym. You're not going to convince us otherwise."

"It's my birthday," Aiden groans. "Do I even get one day without teasing?"

"I think technically it's Luna's *and* your birthday," Carrie says. "So..." She taps a finger to her nose. "That's a no."

"Exactly," his mom says, leaning over and smacking a kiss on his cheek. "That's not how the Blacks do it. Though," she adds when he begins to protest further, "we *can* find a new victim for said teasing. Like," she stage whispers, "why your brother got dumped." A beat. "Again."

"Mom!" Dave snaps. "That's not cool."

"Oh, no," Carrie murmurs. "It's *very* cool. Mostly because you managed to piss off the most patient woman I've ever met with your special brand of bullshit."

He throws up his hands. "All I said was I didn't want to get married."

"*After* you put a ring on her finger," Carrie says, tossing up *her* hands in turn. "Will you marry me to...oh, doh"—she smacks her forehead, a la Homer Simpson—"I guess I changed my mind." She glares at her brother. "Because seriously. You've lost your damned mind. Roxie was the best ever."

"Not to mention that you told her *two* months before the wedding," Kathy exclaims and my eyes go wide. Two months? The man *had* lost his mind. "You really couldn't have *sorted out* your head before all those deposits were put down?"

"His brain doesn't work like that," Ralph chimes in.

Dave's face has gone from bright red to pale, anger morphing into something that looks a little like...

Regret.

Damn. I know that feeling.

"Right," Aiden says, always empathetic, always kind, always knowing when things have gone too far. "I think Dave's had enough, so let's talk about more important things—like why Carrie got so mad at Ralph that she threw out his Han Solo action figure."

Carrie glares. "He deserved it."

"I accidentally dropped one makeup thingy," Ralph cries. "One!"

"It was a Chanel compact," Carrie says. "And it was worth more than your stupid action figure."

"She's got you there, buckaroo," Kathy says.

"Dad!" Ralph complains. "Control your women."

"Seriously," Dave mutters.

Matt looks up from his cup of coffee, shaking his head at his family's shenanigans. "You'd both do better to know there's no such thing as controlling your women."

"Exactly," Kathy says.

"You just learn to ignore them."

"Hey!" Kathy and Carrie say at once.

"And mission accomplished," Aiden murmurs, lips brushing my earlobe again, making me shiver.

When I glance up at him in surprise, he winks, and God, it hits me hard. Because I missed this, missed sitting next to him, the silent language we developed, the silliness between his mom and his siblings, even his dad just sitting on the sidelines, letting them get their tease on, while only occasionally joining in.

And Aiden, stepping in. Navigating the personalities, carefully making sure that no one takes it over the line.

I don't have too many moments like this—most of my and Aiden's free time was spent at the rink—but the handful of family meals I got to attend with the Blacks were *this*.

Boisterous and loud and a bit overwhelming.

But so much better than the silent meals I shared with my brother and dad, the quiet only punctuated by talk of the business or extolling my brother's accomplishments.

Eating with Grams wasn't like that, and it wasn't like this.

It was...cooking interrupted with bites taken bending over the stove, the spoon's contents steaming because we've stolen those bites directly from the pan, "just so we can make sure it tastes right." It was learning new skills, holding tight to the memories of my mom, my sister, making new ones with Grams. It was leaning against the kitchen counter, plates in hand, downing homemade mac n cheese or Seven-Up Cake or cookies so hot out of the oven their chocolate chips were melted, smeared on the corners of our mouths, threatening to drop onto our shirts.

"You're a million miles away," Aiden murmurs.

I blink, realize the conversation has turned to other topics—thankfully for Dave, not about his ability to be a good fiancé. And thankfully for me, Kathy is regaling the table with tales about her garden club instead of shoving pastries down my throat.

They're delicious, yes.

But my stomach is so full I want to unbutton my pants.

And they have an elastic waistband so I won't get any relief there.

"Luns?" he asks, expression growing concerned.

I blink again. "Sorry," I say softly. "Food coma."

He studies my eyes, doesn't say anything. But I have the

feeling he knows I'm lying—or at least that I'm not giving him the full truth.

And it's his birthday.

His family's here.

I'm a complication at best. At worst...

I close my eyes, shove that down, but somehow the words still slip out, "She would have loved to be here."

Gentle green eyes, fingers lacing through mine. "She'd put them in their places easily enough," he murmurs lightly.

I grin. "I think you did pretty good yourself."

"It's wrangling cats." One big shoulder lifts and falls in a shrug. "Evie would have done it as easily as breathing."

Maybe.

She always did better with managing people who weren't my brother and father.

The business. Me. Our friends.

But them?

I don't know if it was because she loved them that they had so much hold over her. Or if it was just a blind spot.

Maybe that's why she put what she put in her will, why she managed to both bequeath a gift *and* a nightmare.

Why desperate has been the defining feature of my last months.

And why I can't seem to find my footing or figure out how best to move forward—should I go against everything I promised I would never do for the greater good or just...let go of what I wanted to do with my family's business and hope to do good elsewhere?

Neither seem like good options.

But only one tugs at my heartstrings...and only one propelled me onto Aiden's doorstep with a marriage contract in hand the night before.

"I should leave," I murmur, "let you enjoy your day with your family."

His eyes lock onto mine again, searching. "I think we have more to talk about."

"It'll hold," I prevaricate.

He tilts his head, not breaking eye contact. "I'm not so sure about that."

"I really should go," I whisper, desperation bubbling back up.

His fingers tighten around mine. "I'm not so sure I want you to."

"Aiden." It's another whisper. Or maybe a plea.

"Stay," he says. "Please."

"I shouldn't." But just the word *please* from him has me wavering, an addict ready for her next hit.

"The universe brought us back together," he says into my ear, the hot puffs of his words glazing my skin. "We shouldn't waste that."

My heart starts thudding. And God, I want that so bad.

But...I *shouldn't.*

"Aiden, I—"

"Oh, Luna!" I jerk, my eyes jumping from Aiden's to Kathy's. "I forgot that since Carrie's husband was called into work and couldn't make it, we have an extra ticket to Aiden's game tonight! You'll come with us, right?"

"I—"

Aiden's fingers tighten around mine again. "Of course, she will."

"Oh, great!" She starts chattering about details and I turn to glare at Aiden.

But he touches my cheek, murmurs, "Come watch me tonight, Luns."

My expression softens, and I nod.
So much for all those *shouldn'ts*.

ELEVEN

Aiden

MY MOM IS MY WINGMAN.

I don't know if that's pathetic.

Or brilliant.

Because Luna couldn't turn her down.

And now I'm eating my pregame snack—a gas station hot dog (don't judge)—and staring down at my phone's screen, a grin playing at the edges of my mouth.

Because my mom just texted me a selfie of her and Luna.

In Grizzlies jerseys.

Christ, I shouldn't like that so much.

"And now I've gotta know why you're smiling so wide," I hear. "Because I don't think it's that the hot dog is extra delicious today."

Okay, so it's less *hear* and more boom.

Because my teammate, Smitty, has exactly one volume level.

And it's loud as fuck, even though he's sitting right next to me.

Case in point? His voice booms across the locker room, drawing everyone's focus.

To me.

Great.

I scowl at him even though I know it will have absolutely no effect—the man has no shame. He's been my teammate from when I first came up in the league—when I secured a roster spot on the Breakers—and he was part of the trade that brought me back to California, to the Grizzlies.

He's also a pain in the ass.

He's loud and brash and never gives an inch. Maybe that's part of the reason I like him so much—he fits in with my family. Hell, the last time my mom was in town for a game Smitty and his—much quieter, but very lovely—wife Kailey ended up out at dinner with my parents and me.

Where my mom declared him and Kailey honorary members of the Black crew.

Something Smitty has taken very seriously.

Case in point? Him leaning over and snatching my phone from my grasp.

He's a big guy, nearing retirement age, but he can still move as quick as lightning.

I don't even have a chance.

He glances down at the unlocked screen and whistles. "Who's this pretty lady?" He lifts his head, holds my gaze, his eyes twinkling with mirth. "And I don't mean your mom."

"Dude," Gray, another teammate, mutters. "Not cool."

He's our captain—quiet but a good leader, always putting in extra effort and time to be his best, both on the ice and in the locker room.

But he doesn't exactly scream open book.

And I'm not sure I've ever made it beyond the outer walls of his personality.

Another one with Shrek-like layers.

That shit is catching around here.

"What?" Smitty says...or rather booms. "A-Man's mom is smoking hot—"

I groan but he isn't fazed in the least.

"—it's just that the girl beside Mrs. Black is next level."

"And now we're doubling down on the not cool," Gray says, rolling his eyes.

I can't say he's wrong—hearing another man say Luna is hot pushes a button inside me I didn't even know I had. Certainly, I've never cared enough about any of the women I've dated over the last decade to be annoyed at the thought of someone else wanting them.

But Smitty noticing *my* Luns? Yup. That certainly pisses me off.

And I don't give a fuck that he's happily married.

Because Luns has made me go full caveman: *Woman mine. Kill all who look at her.*

Only, this is Smitty—pushing the envelope is his super-power—so I table the prehistoric rage that will only have him pestering me more and get back to typical locker room shenanigans—giving each other shit.

"I'm glad you think my mom is hot," I say dryly.

"Notice how he didn't say anything about the woman," Smitty—not wrongly—points out.

Partly because of those caveman feelings...and partly because I don't know how to begin to explain Luna.

A childhood friend? My first love? The woman I want to make...

Mine.

Because that's the truth I feel deep inside me, even after all these years.

But that's also about a dozen steps ahead of where I need to be.

First, I need to get to the truth of the marriage contract. Second, I need to figure out why those shadows are clinging to her eyes—because it's not just her loss of Grams. There's more to the story, more I need to pull out of her, so *third*, I can see about making her mine.

Forever.

I know I'm not going to be content with stolen kisses or hesitant caresses, not going to be content with one night, one week, or even one month.

This is Luns.

And even after a decade apart, nothing's changed for me.

Focusing on the now, I put my hand out for my phone, a silent demand to Smitty to cut the shit and focus on the game ahead of us.

A demand he ignores—both on the cutting the shit part *and* the focusing on our freaking job portion of my warning.

Instead, his eyes go back to the screen and he whistles again. "Someone's got your name on her back, bud."

"What?" I frown.

He tosses my cell over to me and I nearly drop my hot dog trying to catch it.

But I manage to save both.

The picture on my phone's screen, though, has my dog slipping from my fingers, splatting to the floor, ketchup spraying on my skates.

I barely process that.

Because I'm staring at the next photograph from my mom that's popped up, at the playful look that Luna's tossing over her shoulder, gorgeous gray eyes staring directly into the camera, smile wide and beautiful...and my name emblazoned across her shoulders.

Fuck, I like that.

Far more than I should.

"She *is* pretty."

I jump, not realizing that Gray's leaned over, is staring at my phone.

"Jesus Christ," I mutter, locking the screen and shoving it onto the shelf over my head.

"What?" he says and, swear to fuck, but this may be the first time I've ever seen my captain's eyes filled with humor. "I didn't say she was hot." A beat, the corners of his mouth tipping up, just the slightest bit. "Or your mom."

I glare at him. "Fuck off."

He winks then tosses me a towel, jerking his chin in the direction of my skates and the mess I've created.

Scowling, I swipe at my skates, the black mat beneath my feet, then scoop up the remains of my hot dog and walk to the trash can, dumping the rest of my lucky pregame meal inside before tossing the towel into the dirties bin.

Then I go back to my locker, grumbling, "Are we going to stop talking about my personal life and focus on the game?"

"That sounds a lot less fun than giving you shit," Ryan, another teammate, says, his mouth curved into a smile.

Damn.

This shit is catching.

Fucking great.

"Personal lives are on the table?" I ask quietly, knowing that his—mostly because of the woman he loves—might be the most complicated of anyone in this room.

A lifted brow.

A knowing look.

But he doesn't comment further, just goes back to winding tape around his shin guards.

"Yes!" Smitty booms. "Personal lives are *definitely* on the table." He stands up, snagging his jersey. "There are far too many single fuckers on this team, but don't worry"—he yanks the blue and black and white material (a color scheme that, in my opinion, is completely incongruous with the name Grizzlies)—"Matchmaker Smitty is on the case! True love is coming for all of you assholes and I'm going to make sure you're not too stupid to miss it."

"Such inspiring words," Gray mutters, snapping on his helmet.

Smitty opens his mouth.

But our captain is not done talking—and his words have even Smitty shutting up for once.

"Game time, boys," Gray says, shoving on his gloves and heading for the door. "Let's fucking go."

TWELVE

Luna

I'VE GOT a lap full of snacks.

And I'm still stuffed from all of my Molly's treats.

But am I shoving down popcorn by the handful?

Abso-fucking-lutely.

Mostly because I forgot how nerve-wracking it is to watch Aiden play.

He's good, smooth and confident, connecting passes, anticipating what's going to happen next, playing both excellent offense and defense.

But it's fucking terrifying watching him out there.

It's the collisions that have me holding my breath. The sticks flying and pucks shooting across the ice far too fast, hitting the glass and boards, and sometimes the players, with sickening *thunks*. Speaking of which, they all skate at warp speed with gear that doesn't seem thick enough to protect them and—

Carrie bumps her shoulder against mine. "Gonna breathe, kid?"

"I hate watching him," I whisper. After, for the record, chewing my mouthful of popcorn *and* taking a long, slow breath.

"You do?" she asks, eyebrows drawn tightly together.

"I worry about him," I whisper. "A lot of the guys are bigger than him and he might get hurt." Another huge *boom* echoes through the arena, loud enough to be heard over the cheering crowd and I flinch. "I know he's good, that this is his job. But that almost makes it worse. What if he doesn't get hurt, but instead messes up and is upset with himself, and—" I break off, knowing I'm being ridiculous. It's a regular game for a season that's only just barely gotten underway. Yes, Aiden and his team want to win. But this isn't a make-it-or-break it match up.

It's just one game of many.

Of eighty-two, actually.

"Anyway," I murmur. "It's great that he's out there. I'm just...stressed."

Carrie's expression is soft.

But she doesn't call me on my nonsense, only bumps my shoulder again. "You're sweet, Luna. You always have been."

I'm not sure about that.

Especially, considering why I showed up, what I was hoping to do...

No.

I don't want to think about that. Not right now.

I just...want to enjoy tonight and then move along with my problems, leaving Aiden to his uncomplicated life without fathers who are merciless and brothers who don't care and dead grandmothers who meant well but threw a giant curveball into my life that I cannot seem to figure out how to navigate.

...and to Luna, dear. I leave you this personal letter. Read it privately and if you manage to fulfill my request within the next calendar year, then my shares of Smythe Industries are yours to do with as you see fit. Trust the process, break the curse, and know I love you so, so much. But if, after that year, you haven't succeeded, then the shares will revert on a fifty-fifty split to your father and brother.

The bequest shouldn't be legal.

But somehow it is.

Something I know because my brother and father have spent the last eight months fighting it.

And every legal challenge comes back stating her will is iron clad.

"I'm not sure that Aiden would say I'm sweet," I whisper.

She smirks. "I don't think I'd take that bet." A beat. Another bump of her shoulder. "Though, I don't think I want to think about him and you being wicked..." She winks.

I narrow my eyes at her. "*Anyway*," I mutter. "Enough talk about me and your brother. I want to hear about you, about what you've been up to."

"Kids. Work. Husband. Rinse and repeat." She grins when another crash reverberates through the arena and I jump. "I love the kids. Love the husband. And my job on most days. On others I want to tear my hair out strand by strand because my boss is nice, but swear to fuck, he has the man gene where. He. Just. Doesn't. Listen."

I fight a smile.

Then lose my battle when Matt mutters, "We listen. We just don't care."

I giggle.

Carrie sighs, shakes her head.

And we all turn back to the game.

Just in time to watch Aiden jump over the boards and join in on a rush up the ice.

He skates rapidly into the offensive zone, trailing after his teammates as they cross the blue line, not immediately identifiable as a threat.

But he soon makes himself one—skating to the net, picking up a deflected shot, dancing around an opposing player.

I gasp when he's slashed hard, the puck lurching away from him.

Only for a second, though.

Because, just as quickly, he's regained control and is corralling the puck, moving to the goal. The defenseman doesn't make it easy, stepping up, trying to block him, but Aiden doesn't give up—just moves back to give himself some space.

Then he spots it.

Before I do, for sure.

And also before almost everyone on the ice—aside from his teammates.

Because one is streaking in, his stick down and ready...

For the puck that Aiden floats over to him.

The arena full of people all seem to freeze, every one of the twenty-thousand-plus people seeming to hold their breath for one prolonged heartbeat...

The puck flutters toward the tall, bearded player wearing a C on his chest.

He corrals it with a flick of his stick.

And the next flip has it sailing into the back of the net.

A beat of quiet.

Then the red light behind the goal begins to flash and the crowd explodes with cheers so loud my ears hurt. A moment later, the buzzer is joining in on the noise, the team's celebratory song playing.

It's complete and total chaos.

Cacophony.

But it's beautiful.

Almost as beautiful as the looks on the faces of Kathy and Matt, Claire and Ralph and Dave's faces.

The pride.

The joy.

The *love*.

Suddenly, I can't keep up this façade, pretending that Aiden and I are together, not that I just showed up on his doorstep last night with a desperate plan and crazy intentions.

The guilt wells up, clamping onto my lungs, stealing my breath, crawling up my throat.

And then making my eyes burn.

Fuck.

I know I'm not going to be able to hold the tears back.

"Excuse me," I say to Carrie, who looks over at me in shock. "Are you okay?"

"My stomach hurts," I manage to push out as the celebration begins to die. "Too much junk food today. Will you tell your mom that I'll catch up with you all tomorrow?"

"Yes, but," she adds as she stands, starts letting me step over her and into the aisle, "are you sure you don't want me to come with you?"

"I'm fine."

But I'm *not* fine—I don't sound it and she can see that much.

So, when she opens her mouth, I force myself to take a

moment, to keep holding those tears back, for my voice to be steady when I say, "I'll talk to you guys tomorrow, okay?"

And only when she nods do I hurry up the stairs, the sounds of the hockey game below chasing me the entire way.

THIRTEEN

Aiden

ALL I HAVE of her is the contract.

And the knowledge that she lives close.

Because she was staying with her Grams.

But I can't lie—driving an hour just to see the house with the overgrown bushes leading up the walk and the front lawn looking like it needs a serious watering doesn't bode well for solving the perplexing problem of the tornado that is Luna Maybelle.

Evie Maybelle took great pride in her garden.

And Luna spent hours in the yard helping her tend the planter boxes, pull the weeds, trim the edge of the grass to almost laser perfection.

Now it seems...not unloved exactly. An afterthought? A burden that's become too much for one person? Forgotten?

I'm not one hundred percent sure.

I just know it doesn't feel right. So much of this shit doesn't feel right.

Which is almost comical considering the high I was riding last night—we won by three goals—one of which I scored myself and two others that I had an assist on.

And Luna saw...

One of those assists before she left like the hounds of hell were chasing her, nipping at her heels.

At least according to Carrie.

And now my mom is beside herself, thinking that it's something she did—for example, force-feeding Luna pastries in order to put meat on her bones—so she's been blowing up my phone with ever more fretful texts.

Until, I lied to her and said that Luna had called and she wanted to meet up.

That calmed the worst of the stress, gave me time to Google map the shit out of Rockfield, trying to remember the exact street that Luna's grandma used to live on.

It's been a decade since I was here, and that was only a couple of times.

Occasionally we hung at my house, but mostly, Luna and I hung at the rink.

Considering that she and I lived and breathed our sports.

Which begs the question—why did she stop skating?

Once, it was everything to her.

Another curiosity. Another puzzle piece. Another layer.

I exhale, scrub a hand over my face, then reach for the door handle, popping it open and hoping against hope that the clunker in the driveway is her car.

But, considering how it's been going since I walked off the ice and got the bad news that she took off, I'm not holding my breath.

She can't hide forever, though.

Next stop is Smythe Industries to talk to her dad.

Which will be...unpleasant if he's the same old codger who

occasionally deigned to show up for one of her competitions, on his phone the whole time, a perpetual scowl in place.

Fun. Fun.

Thankfully, I have another plan to work through before I have to deal with that shitshow.

I slam the door, move around the front of my car, and start heading up the driveway.

God, the flowers are the same bright and cheerful—colorful explosions that almost assault my eyes with their vivid blooms.

But again, they're overgrown.

Not the well-controlled beds that Grams had spoken of— and showed pictures of—with such pride. Even the little sign next to the door, declaring all are welcome is faded, the paint chipping away.

The mat is different, newer, as though someone is making an effort—a simple welcome emblazoned on the rough brown material. I stop, my toes just on top of it, and exhale.

Then I jab at the doorbell.

The chime echoes inside, and I hear footsteps coming toward me.

I brace for disappointment, for having to track her down somewhere else.

There's a *click* of the lock disengaging, the handle turns, and...

The door pulls open.

"Aiden!" Luna gasps.

God, she's beautiful.

And I know I should demand answers, demand explanations...

I don't do either.

I just step over the threshold, nudge her back, and slam and lock the door behind me.

"What are you—?"

I don't let her finish the question.

I *can't.*

It's like every instinct in me is screaming, telling me I won't get anywhere trying to push her. Or maybe...it's that every instinct in me is screaming at me to claim what is mine.

Whatever the reason, I just wrap an arm around her waist, tug her against me.

Then I bend and slant my mouth over hers.

She goes still for a long moment, for long enough for me to think this is absolutely the wrong fucking move.

Then it's like something snaps inside her.

She becomes a flurry of movement, of intensity, of wild woman whom I have no hope of containing.

And I don't want to.

Instead, I heft as she jumps, grabbing the bottoms of her thighs, encouraging her to wrap her legs around my waist. And I sure as fuck don't stop kissing her, just walk her toward the stairs as she moans, our tongues dancing, her pelvis grinding against mine.

"Aiden," she gasps when I let her breathe, when I kiss my way along her throat.

My toes hit the bottom stair and I lift my foot, intending to find somewhere horizontal to finish what we started yesterday.

As usual, Luna has other plans.

She snakes her hand down between us.

I hiss as her fingers hit my bare skin, as they slip beneath the waistband of my pants, my underwear, and wrap around my cock.

"Christ, Luns," I groan, thrusting into her hand.

Because she squeezes tightly. Because she starts stroking fast and furious and—

Dangerously.

As in, I'm already dangerously close—the stress of her

disappearing act, the interruption yesterday morning, the absolute certainty that she's mine...they all pile on top of each other and send me dangerously spinning toward the edge.

I spin and sit on the third stair from the bottom, dragging her down on top of me.

She doesn't stop stroking me, doesn't falter in her rhythm.

At least until I grab the hem of her tee and yank it up and over her head.

Another lacy bra.

Lush tits I need to bury my face in, need to lick and stroke, suck and kiss.

I reach behind her and flick open the clasp, freeing them.

But she's freeing me too, opening the button on my jeans, dragging the zipper down. A tug has my cock out and even though I try to stop her—intent on those breasts—she shimmies down my body and sucks me deep.

"Fuck!" I shout, hand diving into her hair.

A grin, the hard length of me sliding out of her mouth with a soft *pop!* "Yeah, big shot. You like that?"

I tug lightly at her hair. "Yeah, sweetheart," I murmur. "Which begs the question—why the fuck did you stop?"

A stroke. An innocent look that I don't buy in the least. "Oh, did you want me to keep going?"

I growl and reach for her.

But she darts back. "Fine," she teases, hand moving again. "Fine, I guess I'll keep going." Then she's bending again, dragging the flat of her tongue along my erection, pink lips parting at the top and taking me into that hot, slick mouth.

She swallows me down, so deeply I bob against the back of her throat.

I curse again, control rapidly disintegrating.

Tight fingers, a confident tongue, plump lips.

Christ, this woman makes me insane.

I thrust up carefully with my hips, bobbing against the back of her throat again, groaning when she swallows me down with a moan that vibrates through my shaft.

She pulls, *oh so slowly*, back, the head of my cock resting on her bottom lip, her words a damp glaze when she orders, "Behave."

And my control splinters.

"Oh no, baby," I rasp. "There's no fucking way I'm going to behave."

FOURTEEN

Luna

ONE SECOND, I'm confidently in control.

The next...

I'm suddenly naked and bare-assed on the stairs, my legs shoved wide, a big, bearded hockey player between my legs.

He licks me without quarter, exploiting every single pleasure-inducing spot he found yesterday.

My clit, the sensitive part of my labia, the top of my entrance...

Inside.

With fingers and tongue and—

I clutch at his shoulders, grind myself against him. "Oh, God!"

And just that quickly, I go from riding high of power to reveling in the strength of his.

Broad shoulders, calloused fingertips, and that beard that is the sweetest type of abrasion I've ever experienced.

Only, I don't want to come without him this time.

And I'm all of three seconds away from forgetting that, from letting the wonderful things he's doing to me push me over the edge...

But—

Aiden.

I'm finally with Aiden.

And I don't want to fall apart again—

Not alone.

Not without him.

So, I hold off my orgasm, the flickers I can already feel beginning to flutter through my pussy, clamping down on his fingers. It's so close. So *fucking* close.

Gritting my teeth, I reach for his shoulders, summoning no little amount of strength—some might even say it's actually a *herculean* amount of strength—and I heave. "Up," I rasp, pushing him back. "Inside me," I order.

I'm fully aware that he's so much bigger and stronger than me, so if he truly wanted to fight me on this, he could. Easily. But I'm also fully aware that he's just as turned on as me. So, he doesn't fight me—much—just giving my pussy one more long lick before crawling up my body.

"Inside me," I demand again.

He gives me a heart-stopping smile—God, he is seriously the sexiest man I've ever seen—reaches into the back pocket of his jeans, and pulls out his wallet. He opens it, tugs out a condom, tearing the packet open with his teeth. A moment later, he's rolling it down the length of his erection, protecting us both without me having to ask.

Which just adds to his sexiness.

And a moment after that...

I moan, my head falling back against the stairs with a *thunk*.

"Careful, sweetheart," he murmurs, fingers lacing into my

hair, cushioning my skull, the head of his cock notched at my entrance, barely an inch of his length inside me.

"More," I command, squirming against the pleasurable intrusion—big and hard and yet not nearly enough.

He doesn't argue, just flexes his hips, gaining another inch inside me.

I moan again, and this time he joins me, his eyes going to half-mast, sweat glistening on his forehead, the muscles on his chest and shoulders and abs standing out in sharp relief—

"More?" he asks.

"More," I say again as I wrap a leg around his waist, arching my back, rocking my pelvis, my hips meeting his careful forward movements and allowing him to sink even deeper, so deep that I've gained all of him, that I'm so full of him I can barely speak, barely think, barely move.

"Good?" he asks.

"Big," I push out, the word a struggle because I've never felt so full, so possessed, so under a man's control.

He grins. "You can handle it."

My pussy begins to relax and even as I begin testing the intrusion of him, hips continuing to rock gently against the impressive length of his erection, the sass that's always a deep well inside me makes itself known. It's a miracle I can feel something aside from *full*, something aside from the micro-currents of sensation transforming into sparks of pleasure.

I know it won't be long now.

So, I take advantage of my brain working for the moment.

And draw on that sass.

"As long as *you* know how to handle it," I tease him.

Unfortunately, the joke's power is undermined a bit by the fact that I'm a little breathless and that I'm grinding against him and also that my eyes are practically rolling into the back of my head because Aiden is beautiful and wonderful and his dick feels fucking *incredible*.

His grin turns wolfish, sending spasms through me. "What makes you think I can't handle it, tiny tornado?"

"I don't know," I huff out, rocking faster, the sparks of pleasure increasing in magnitude, dragging me closer and closer to the edge. "The fact that you're packing a weapon down there?"

He chuckles and...yeah, I'm going to come.

And the man isn't even fucking me yet.

What the hell is happening right now?

My lungs work, drawing in staccato breaths. My pulse hammers through my veins, pounds against the backs of my ears. My mind is spinning, trying to make sense of the cacophony of sensations.

And then I decide...

Quantifying it doesn't matter.

Comparing it to anything I've experienced before won't work.

This is *Aiden*.

It will always be *more* with him.

And that's always been the problem.

A bolt of worry slices through me, honing down the sharp edges of my desire, "I—"

But then he speaks, his voice husky, his cock inside me twitching, his lips *oh so close* to mine, "Well then, my tiny tornado, I think you're about to find out."

He pairs the last word with a thrust that steals my breath away, and I arch back against the stairs, my head dropping to one of the treads again, my legs wrapping tightly around his hips.

We both groan.

"Good," he grunts.

"Great," I correct on a moan.

"The fucking best."

"Yes!"

To that and the sensations rippling through me as he thrusts hard and fast, driving into me, over and over again.

It's not anything like what I've had before—slow caresses and a slow build, gentle strokes and long, drugging kisses.

I liked that. Thought it was *everything* I liked.

This though—

It's rough. It's intense. It's almost overwhelming.

It's...

The fucking best.

More than I anticipated, more than I dreamed I could have, more than I think I can take.

Except, somehow with Aiden I *know* I can handle it.

Can handle even more.

And he doesn't fail to give it to me.

"Oh, my God!" I cry as he drives harder. "Oh, my—"

It's there. *Right* there. Right freaking *there*—

"Aiden!"

I come apart and I barely have the chance to watch his gorgeous face as he does the same before my vision blurs and I'm riding the waves of my pleasure, sinking into the glorious oblivion, going limp and lazy and lax.

I stay that way for what might be seconds or hours or decades.

But it only takes one sentence from him to have that disappearing like so much smoke.

He brushes his lips over mine then lifts his head, eyes locking on to mine.

"Now, sweetheart, you're going to tell me what's really going on with the marriage contract."

FIFTEEN

Aiden

SO...MAYBE not the *best* time to ask mere minutes after the best orgasm of my life—especially if I want another one at some point in the near future.

And I fucking *do* want another one, a hundred, a thousand more.

But I've been going on instinct from the moment I got in my car and drove over here.

I'm just...going to let go, ride this ride, and hopefully I'll get to the truth of the matter.

And hopefully it'll be sooner rather than later.

Hopefully, she won't kick my ass out to the curb and disappear from my life again.

"Tell me Luns," I press.

She closes her eyes, turns her head away, her body going taut beneath mine.

Damn stubborn woman.

I exhale silently then pull out, scooping her up, and climbing the stairs, doing my best to remember where her room was.

Each of the doors along the hall are open and I can see that each contains a stack of boxes.

All except for the last.

That door is closed.

I turn the handle, push inside, and freeze at the spartan furnishings.

A single bed, a nightstand, a narrow, beat-up dresser.

Luna's family has money, a *lot* of money. The family business was doing well when we were kids and I've heard no shortage of news stories about it expanding over the last few years. Hell, I think it even went public during the first quarter of *this* year.

So, while I can understand her keeping this place—she always talked about how much she preferred staying here, that it was more home than the house she shared with her brother, her father—I don't understand why it looks like this, don't understand why this is the only room on this floor with anything aside from boxes inside it.

Why this is the only room that shows any sign of being lived in.

But living like this—in a packed-up house, her life reduced to a sparse bedroom...

It doesn't make sense.

And it drives home exactly how little I know of the Luna of today, of the Luna who knocked on my door, the Luna who allowed herself to be swept along with the craziness that is my family, soaked up the day, and then...ran.

I settle her on the mattress, go to one of the two closed doors in the space and get lucky on my first guess, finding the bathroom.

I take care of the condom, put myself to rights, and wash my hands.

Then I slip back out into the bedroom.

Since Luna is still sitting there, seemingly lost in her thoughts, I head back out to the hall, snagging her clothes from the various places I tossed them—the banister, near the front door, halfway down the stairs—then bring them back up to her.

She tugs them on, her movements jerky and robotic.

But she's avoiding my eyes.

Which tells me enough.

I'm not going to like what she's holding back.

She pulls on one sock, the other, then pops to her feet. "You should go."

I sink down onto the bed, lace my fingers through hers, then tug her back down beside me. "Luns," I warn.

She pulls against but I hold her fast, and I wait...

For a long fucking time.

For her to stop fighting against my hold, to stop avoiding my eyes, to finally just give in and look at me.

"Luns," I murmur. "Will you just trust me enough to talk to me?"

She's tense—so fucking tense—but my question has her releasing a shuddering breath. "You know that I trust you," she finally whispers.

But she doesn't keep talking.

Doesn't clue me into what's creating such turmoil.

"So, why won't you talk to me?" I ask when long minutes pass without her cluing me in.

"Because it's a long, fucked-up story."

I glance around the room then turn back to her with my brows lifted and shrug. "Do I look like I have anywhere more important to be, tiny tornado?"

She stays still and I hold my breath, waiting, hoping, praying to whatever gods exist that she lets me in.

Then she exhales…

And, thank fuck, the words start coming.

"I didn't want this to touch you," she whispers. "But I brought it to your doorstep."

I frown.

But she keeps going. "I knew I shouldn't go to your condo, knew I shouldn't have tracked you down in the first place, but I was desperate and thought it was my only option and—" She sighs. "Obviously, I wasn't thinking clearly."

"Because you came to my place?" I touch her cheek, try to coax a smile out of her. "I mean, yeah it was the middle of the night, but at least you brought cake."

Her mouth curves, but it's an empty gesture.

"No," she whispers. "Because I thought it was actually something we should do. Because I thought it would fix everything."

That settles heavy on my amusement, tamping it down. "How, Luns?" I ask. "How can marrying me fix anything?"

She shakes her head, eyes sliding closed. "It doesn't matter," she murmurs. "Because it's not going to happen."

I leave the second part alone, along with the insane thought that maybe making this woman mine in every way might not be the worst idea—that's the crazy talking—but anyway, the first is more important right now.

I cup her jaw. "Try that bullshit with someone else, sweetheart."

"It's not bull—"

I turn her head toward me, my eyes locking onto hers. "Then tell me what getting married would fix."

Her eyes drift away.

"Luns," I warn.

They come back, the gray depths conflicted, an intense storm raging in her gaze.

But eventually—and fucking *finally*—she answers me,

"Because it will save Grams's legacy."

SIXTEEN

Luna

I WANT to claw the words back from the air, shove them deep down so they never have the chance to see the light of day.

So Aiden never hears them.

Just...move on. Move *out*.

Put the past behind me and forget whatever crazy notion I had that I could fix everything.

Because it will *ruin* everything else.

And Aiden is too good to have that happen to him, to deal with me, with my family, with all the business can destroy.

It was delusional to think I could save it, could do something better with it.

I'm just Luna. I don't have any business experience. I don't have connections with the board like my brother John has. I don't have the support of the executive staff like my dad has. I don't have both like Grams did.

I'm just a dumb girl who wants to fulfill the big dreams I used to sit in this bedroom and write about.

"I'm gonna need you to explain, Luns."

"I barely understand it myself."

He sighs, fingers flexing slightly, holding me in place with his touch, with his intense green eyes. "Then let's start at the beginning and talk it out."

"Grams read my diaries."

His brow furrows, but he doesn't comment except to say, "Go on."

"I wrote in them a lot—silly stuff like what happened at school or my feelings for you"—my mouth hitches up, heart skipping a beat when I see those green eyes gentle, when he smiles back at me—"but as I got older, it was a way for me to decompress. I'd write about my experiences at college and the professors who drove me crazy or the classes I loved, and later, after I graduated and began to learn more about the business— the good, the bad, and worse, the ugly—I would write about what I wanted to do with Smythe," I whisper. "What we *could* do so much better."

"Like what?" he asks quietly.

I suck in a breath, release it slowly. "Did you know that we're one of the few companies in the United States that produces insulin?"

He shakes his head. "No, sweetheart."

"We do, but we don't do it right."

"What do you mean, Luns?"

Another breath. Then...I just let the words flow. "Do you know that the original patent from Dr. Banting for the first formulary of insulin was sold for a dollar because he wanted everyone to have access the life-saving drug? And do you know that insulin today costs between two to four dollars per vial to produce but costs Americans an average of two hundred and fifty dollars? *And* do you know that same vial used to cost twenty-one dollars—twenty-one dollars!—in 1996?" I take a breath because my heart rate is speeding, frustration at the injustice—and my small part in it—bringing the words forward fast and furious. "Americans pay ten times more for insulin than other countries, and they die because they ration their insulin because they can't afford it, risk their lives for a disease they didn't ask for, a disease that is a lifelong burden to manage."

My throat goes tight, and I slam my eyes closed, dangerously close to crying.

Again.

Because until I saw a video online, I had no idea what my family's company was doing.

What I was part of.

And then I dove headfirst into researching, into discovering all that I could about the industry my family's business was in...until I had a solid plan for moving forward in a way that's still profitable, but doesn't trample innocent people. Only, when I brought that plan to my brother, my father, the board...

Not one person cared—or they didn't care more than what Smythe was already providing their bank accounts with their current structure.

A cut to profits, no matter how slight, was unacceptable.

I can't pretend to be perfect and innocent in this—I benefited from Smythe's power too. It paid for my skating, my schooling, my rent, my car, my clothes. Until I moved home and had my epiphany, anyway.

Then that door was shut to me, the spigot turned off.

And even then I still benefit from Grams leaving me this house, because I have no school loans or car payment. Me struggling paycheck to paycheck without those debts is nothing compared to what others go through.

It's hard, but I can make it work.

Plus, I don't want that money—not when it's been built off the backs of innocent people.

I tell Aiden all of that, watching his face change, pride shining in his emerald eyes.

But I can't let that sink in.

Because there's more.

And I love Grams, but I cannot believe that she put what she put in her will, that she was playing with people's lives...all because she wanted me to get fucking married within a calendar year.

Which is just another reason why my showing up on Aiden's doorstep was incredibly fucking selfish.

"Sweetheart," he says softly when the words have dried up, his hand still gentle on my cheek, eyes searching mine, as though he knows my thoughts shifted and he's trying to ferret the new ones out. "You've been doing your best, but it's not easy being alone. Don't discount that."

"Two and a half billion dollars," I whisper, not able to sit in that pride, to think about my struggles, not when my family is responsible for so much pain. "That's how much we made on insulin last year. And that was forty percent more than the one-point-six billion from the year before. Off of a patent that was available for a dollar," I say, feeling sick. "Yes, we spend R&D money on new formularies, but that has paid for itself a thousand fold over just the last few years. So why are people rationing here when people in other countries get these meds for free? Why are they struggling when we're raking it in hand over fist? Why are we so fucking greedy when we can actually do some fucking good *and* still have plenty of money to pad our bank accounts?" I clamp my lips together and breath slowly, steadily. "So you clearly see why my dad and brother aren't happy with me right now."

"Yeah, I bet." He touches my cheek. "But you're passionate

about this, Luns. Something Grams clearly saw that if she read anything close to what you were speaking about in your diaries."

My mouth hitches up. "I may have written a more than a few pages in my raging."

"So, she did see it?"

I nod.

"Then what happened?"

I rub the throb in my temple. "I was finishing up my degree —I went back for my MBA because I wanted to contribute something to the company, but when I was"—I do finger quotes —"*radicalized*, according to my brother and dad, they made it their jobs to cut me out of mine. I was shut out of meetings, left out of the loop on conference calls, slowly pushed out of the way. Then Grams got sick and I was too focused on her to fight for my place, especially when she got sick enough that she needed to move in with my dad and I followed suit, not wanting her to be alone."

He frowns.

"What?"

"But why couldn't you both stay here?"

"Termites," I whisper. "A fucking tub fell through the living room ceiling and she needed some place safe to live...and we tented, did all the necessary repairs, but she never got well enough to move home."

"Shit, Luns," he mutters. "I'm sorry."

"I know."

I exhale. "I took my eye off the ball. They quietly hired someone else in my place and suddenly I was stuck without a paycheck. Then when I didn't fall in line, I also lost my connection to the family coffers and thus, I lost what little power I had to force them to do anything. I didn't want the dirty money, but it was the only strength I had."

He frowns.

But I keep going. I *have* to.

"Grams left me some life insurance money," I say. "It was enough to pay the property and inheritance taxes, covered me for utilities and food for a while, and I found a job that I really enjoy at a nonprofit that means I'm doing okay money-wise." I sigh. "But I haven't found any clear way forward with Smythe, any way to make all my anger at the injustices they commit to actually *mean* something."

He takes my hand. "It's not easy to fight against a company as big as Smythe."

"That's just it." I find my fingers tightening on his, my anger bubbling anew—but it's not just at my dad, my brother, the board, the corporate greed.

It's at Grams too.

Because she could have fixed this if only she hadn't made that damned request.

"*What's* it, sweetheart?"

"She had the tools to fight them. And she offered to give them to me."

He frowns. "And you didn't want them or—?"

"No." I shift closer, needing him to understand. "I wanted them so *freaking* bad."

"Then why—?"

"Because in order to use them, she said I had to get married."

SEVENTEEN

Aiden

I KNOW my mouth is hanging open.

But if anyone would have asked me how Luna would finish the explanation she was giving me, there is absolutely no fucking way I could have predicted it would have ended with Grams demanding she get married.

I should have—considering the whole middle of the night *Let's get married!*—but I didn't.

Hockey has addled my brain.

Or maybe the best orgasm of my life did.

Po-tay-toes. Po-tah-toes.

"I don't think I understand," I tell her.

"I didn't either," she murmurs, shoving her hair out of her face and sinking back down onto the bed. "It just...Grams had opinions and she always thought she knew what was right"—a half smile on her face—"don't know where I got that from, am I right?"

She's joking, so that's something.

A hell of a lot better than the grief and betrayal and hurt from before.

"Stubborn and Maybelle go together like peanut butter and jelly," I tell her softly, recalling a long-ago memory of something I heard Grams say.

A soft smile. "She used to look so damned proud of herself when she said that."

I touch her cheek. "I remember." Then wait for her to go on.

Then wait some more.

She sighs. "I'm not explaining this well."

"I admit that there are a few key details that are missing, but I think I'm starting to put the pieces together." I tuck her hair behind her ear. "What are the tools she didn't give you?"

"Her stocks in Smythe," she says. "Combined with my small sliver they would give me the controlling share."

My eyes go wide as I realize what that means.

"I can fix the company," she whispers. "Or at least put enough pressure on my brother, my dad, the rest of the board in order to make it better. But instead of signing them over to me, she told me that they would only be mine if I was married within twelve months."

And she died...eight months ago.

Fuck.

That doesn't leave Luna much time.

"I put it off." A wince. "I admit I did. I mean, it was crazy and when my dad and brother found out what she was offering they tried to fight it. But the lawyers say it's ironclad. She's not forcing me to get married, merely bestowing a gift on me if I do." She sighs. "It's a mess—was, *is* a mess, and I spent too much time dithering about what to do. I mean, at first I was so busy with arrangements and forcing myself to just get up and out of bed that I didn't even consider it. Then I did, but—of

MARRIED TO NUMBER 22   103

course—I couldn't get *married*. That would be insane. So, I resolved that I just needed to content myself with helping in other ways—my work at the nonprofit, selling my shares and donating to the proceeds to charity. Plus, I have this place. I have my job. That's so much more than so many other people."

"So what changed?"

She pushes off the bed, moves to the stack of boxes shoved into the corner and pulls out a battered blue-floral-printed box. "I found this." She comes back over, sets the container next to me and opens the lid.

My heart pulses as I recognize my teenage boy handwriting scrawled all over the long notes we used to write each other.

She had a locker at the rink, gave me the combination to her lock.

I'd leave the notes in her left skate.

And she'd put ones for me in the right one.

"God," I whisper, pulling out one of the intricately folded papers. "I forgot about these."

"Me too," she says. "At least until I moved back in here and started to unpack."

"Unpack?" I tease lightly, glancing around the room filled with boxes, thinking about the row of rooms similarly adorned I walked by earlier.

She narrows her eyes at me. "I've been busy."

I tug at her ponytail, wink, then I dig a little deeper—finding ribbons she won and medals, judge's scoresheets and a CD burned with music from one of her skating programs.

And I wonder again...why did she stop skating? Why did she push me away so hard when I left for juniors?

We could have kept in touch. She could have kept competing.

Instead, it's like she slammed the door on that chapter of her life and moved on.

I open my mouth to ask her...

But then I find the photographs.

And, Jesus, we were young. So young and I was clearly obsessed—staring at her like she hung the sun.

During that time I thought she did.

That's why it hurt so much why she broke up with me.

And why, I suppose, if I'm thinking about it now, I closed the door on that part of my life and deliberately moved forward. If my life was hockey and only hockey, I didn't have time to think about missing her.

Which worked...terribly at first and then reasonably well as the years went on.

But I always had that itch between my shoulder blades, that hole inside me, that well of loneliness.

Because I didn't have Luna.

God, I'm an idiot.

I should have stayed in touch with her, should have sought her out anytime in the last decade, should have done so many damned things differently—she wouldn't have been alone when Grams passed, wouldn't have dealt with her brother and dad alone, wouldn't have—

"Aiden?" she asks quietly and I shove down the turmoil, the regret.

There's no going back.

But I can go forward, can make sure to not waste any more time.

Just thinking those words eases the hold on my lungs, fills in that gap deep in my heart. I can do things differently from here on out.

"I remember this day," I say, pointing to a shot of us sitting at a table in the rink with our textbooks open, a pair of hot chocolates in front of us.

"Yeah," she murmurs, stroking a finger over our smiling faces. "That day was the first time I kissed you."

I feel my cheeks heat, thinking about her taking my hand, drawing me around to a shadowy corner of the rink, and surprising me—like usual—with a kiss. "I wasn't very good at it, was I?" I say, lifting her hand and pressing my lips to her palm.

"I don't think either of us were." She sighs then rests her head on my shoulder. "Though, I'm happy to say I think we got better at it."

"A *lot* better," I agree. Then, even though I hate to, I gently tug us back into the future. "So, you found this and the contract was inside?"

A long pause. Then she nods without lifting her head. "Yeah. I found the paper, the notes, our pictures...and I was just so lonely." A shaky breath. "And admittedly desperate because time was running out and I'd lose my chance at Grams's shares, at fulfilling all those dreams for Smythe. But was I really just going to go out and marry a stranger?"

I don't like that.

Not at fucking all.

Though, before I can say something stupid—like no fucking way are you going to be with someone else—she keeps talking.

"Then I saw a highlight of a Grizzlies game, couldn't believe it was *you* on the screen, that you were close after all this time, back here in California, same as me." She lifts her head, mouth gently curved. "And I remembered the time in the rink, the kisses, the boy you were. So...I admit that I did some unscrupulous things to track down your address—"

My eyebrows fly up and I make a mental note to get her to expand on that later.

Right now, there are more important things to focus on.

"I drank a little wine for courage, picked up that cupcake, and came to your house."

I hold my breath.

"And you were *you*," she murmurs. "My Aiden of old, except all grown up. Beautiful, sweet, and still with that yummy ass—"

My laughter bursts out of me.

Then I sober when she touches my cheek. "And I knew if I told you everything you'd find a way to fix it. But I also knew within a few minutes with you that I couldn't ask that of you. Jesus, Aiden." She groans, shoves a hand through her hair. "You're living your dream! You made it to the NHL. You *freaking* did it. And what the hell am I doing? Popping back into your life, trailing bullshit in my wake."

"You're right," I say.

Her head flies up, eyes going wide.

Hurt dancing through the gray depths.

I cup her cheek.

Press my lips to her forehead, feeling my next words with absolutely certainty.

"Because I *am* going to fix it, Luns."

"Wh-what?"

"We're getting married, sweetheart."

EIGHTEEN

Luna

I STARE at my reflection in the mirror, panic bubbling beneath the surface.

It's been three days since I confessed everything to Aiden and I've barely stopped to think.

Because if I *start* thinking then I'll start panicking and then where will I be?

Running the other way so I don't mess up Aiden's life?

Letting go of this boy, this man, a completely different kind of dream?

I exhale, shoring myself up, even as I know that I'm not going to walk away, that I'm going through with his plan anyway.

Because I want to change things at Smythe.

And because...I want Aiden for however long he lets me have him. I want to stock up on memories, store them away for later, for when I'm alone again, for when the Maybelle Curse strikes.

"He knows the truth," I whisper to my reflection.

And he came up with the plan.

He and the Grizzlies are playing in Vegas tomorrow, having flown there directly after their home game last night. Today he's picking up a marriage certificate after practice then will meet me at the airport. We'll hit his hotel room, get changed, and then...do the ultimate Vegas thing—

Get married by Elvis.

Then lawyers and stocks and Smythe and...soaking up all that is Aiden.

Well, the last part is my addition.

The rest of it—all him. And it all sounded so simple when he brought it up, an easy checklist to make our way through.

Until I remembered what would eventually happen.

The Maybelle Curse.

Why me letting him go years ago wasn't purely selfless—yes, he needed the freedom to pursue his dreams, but also yes, it's only a matter of time before it all goes wrong...same as it's gone wrong for every woman in my family.

I close my eyes, shove that away.

I don't want to think about having to let him go. Back to his life.

To his family.

Don't want to think about being alone again.

"Ugh," I mutter, stabbing the wand of my mascara into the tube and twisting with vigor. It makes me feel better, at least until I hear an ominous crack. I freeze. God, I don't need to be wasting money on stupid shit right now, especially after I bought a plane ticket (refusing to let Aiden purchase one for me) and a dress and...a likely ill-advised scrap of fabric the purports to be lingerie.

But everything with Aiden is complicated.

The one thing that isn't?

Sex.

That's simple and feels good—okay, it feels *great*—and it's something I can give him that isn't going to be a pain in the ass.

No complications.

Just the two of us.

So maybe the lingerie was less ill-advised and more... leaning into the things that make sense.

Shaking my head at myself, I carefully loosen the lid of my mascara and focus on the present.

On real life.

This is simply a means to an end—with Aiden doing me a giant solid—and I'm going to do my best to return the favor, to make it good, to make sure it doesn't explode in his face, to make certain the shrapnel of my life doesn't wound him.

I'll take care of things while he's on the road, give him mind-blowing orgasms when he's home, and we're friends, lovers. We've always gotten along, always had a great time together. I'll make sure that doesn't change either.

Then, eventually...I'll set him free.

And no, I'm not acknowledging how much the thought of that hurts already.

How much more it will hurt when I get more time with him.

My heart pulses and I clench my teeth together.

Before it goes bad, I will set him free.

"Like a fucking butterfly," I mutter dryly as I shove the rest of my makeup into my toiletry bag then bring it to my suitcase, stowing it, and zipping everything closed.

That makes this all feel real, but at least my mental pep talk means that I'm not going to run screaming into the heels. I can't, not just for me, but also for what I want to do.

So, I make it downstairs without incident, heading for the front door.

Unfortunately, that's where *without incident* ends.

Because just as I'm reaching for the door, there's a knock on the other side.

No. Someone's *pounding* on the other side.

And there are only two people who think they have the right to announce their presence like this, who think they have the right to *me*.

My father.

And John—my brother.

"Dammit," I whisper, pushing my suitcase to the side, parking it against the wall. I drop my tote onto the floor next to it.

And then I shore myself up.

I'll deal with them.

I always do.

The pounding lets up for a half a second then starts anew, thankfully annoying me enough that I'm running on rage as I flick the lock, twist the handle, and then yank open the door. "What?" I snap, seeing it's my brother, and thank fuck for small miracles, that he's alone.

"We need to go to the office," he snaps. "Immediately."

My hackles go up and I grind my teeth together so I don't snap at him, so I don't *throttle* him. "I'm busy today," I grit out, and at least my tone is neutral. "Want to clue me in on what you need?"

"There's a board meeting and a vote." He jerks his hand impatiently. "You need to be there for it."

"Something I'd maybe know about if I wasn't pushed out of the family business?" I ask dryly.

He jerks again, this time with his whole body. "This shit again?" He sniffs. "I thought you didn't want any part of our *dirty money*." A sneer. "I was just doing as you asked, remember?"

Convenient he only did it because it made him easier to further his agenda and shut down mine.

But he's not wrong.

I wanted out of the family business...at least until Grams dropped her bombshell.

But God, I just don't have the energy to deal with his bull-shit today.

Which means I need to do he wants me to do so I can move on with my plans.

I stifle a sigh. "What time is the meeting?"

"Three."

I glance at my phone. It's two and my flight is at six. "I can give you an hour," I tell him. "Any longer and I'm out the door."

"Fine." He juts his chin toward his car. "I'll drive."

I stifle my snort. Yeah, that's not going to fucking happen. I'm not going to be conveniently trapped. "I have things to finish up here," I tell him. "I'll meet you at the office."

A long look and I watch the battle in his eyes.

He can push this, can try to force me to ride with him.

But he'll lose that fight.

Or he can take the small victory and live to control me another day.

"Don't be late," he snaps.

I resist taking the bait, grind my teeth together, and wait for him to leave.

Then I go back inside, take a moment to breathe, to shore up my spine.

And...I prepare to face my family.

My nightmare.

NINETEEN

Aiden

I KNOW the moment I spot her coming down the escalators that something is seriously wrong.

But I also know she's here, so it likely doesn't involve me.

Or not completely anyway.

She wheels her suitcase behind her, face a mask of icy calm that I want to chip through.

She's intent on the exit and I realize she hasn't spotted me so I hurry over, wrapping my fingers around the handle of her luggage.

"Wh—?" She starts, then I watch some of the ice melt.

Without me having to break my way through.

I can't lie, that feels fucking great.

"Hi, tiny tornado," I murmur, brushing the backs of my knuckles over her cheek. "I take it your day didn't go smoothly?"

A furrow forms between her eyebrows. "How do you—?"

I snag the suitcase from her, tug the tote off her arm and hang it over my shoulder.

Then I take her hand. "I can tell, Luns."

Her nose wrinkles. "I don't want to talk about it."

Considering we're in a busy airport about to catch a taxi down to The Strip, I don't push it. This isn't the time or place. We can talk later. Right now, she's here. "How are the feet?"

The furrow deepens, head tilting to the side as she studies me. "What do you mean?"

"We're getting hitched tonight, Luns," I say, drawing her toward the exit. "Are those tootsies getting cold?"

She glances up at me, lips twitching. "Tootsies?"

But the last of the ice melts away as I squeeze her hand, say, "Yup. *Tootsies.*"

A snort. "They're toasty warm." She lifts a sneaker-clad foot. "And warmer still because we're in the desert."

Laughter in my chest. "Thankfully, the autumn nights are pleasant?"

"Exactly."

We pause at the end of the taxi queue, inching forward as the crowd snakes around the metal barriers up to the line of waiting cabs. It's noisy, everyone excited to start their weekend, to party and drink and fuck themselves into oblivion.

All the Vegas things.

Blow money. Get lucky.

And leave it all in Sin City.

"I feel like I need to say again that you don't have to do this," she murmurs and the excitement surrounding us almost drowns out her voice.

I stifle a sigh—stubborn woman. I thought we'd already talked this shit through.

Or that I'd promised to fix it, battled her stubborn streak, and came out on top.

Because she agreed.

Because she's here.

I should have known it wouldn't be that easy.

"Luns," I say quietly.

She takes a long time to look up at me.

But eventually those gray storm-cloud eyes come to mine, hold.

And I see it's not stubbornness. Her gaze is filled with worry, with guilt, with fear, with hurt—and beneath all of that, I realize, my heart skipping a beat—with longing. It's the same longing inside me, the same longing that was a constant ache after I left, that never really went away even when life took us on separate journeys.

Because I didn't have her.

Now I do.

Now she's in my life.

She thinks this is something temporary, a hurdle to clear to get those stocks, a means to an end before we'll part again.

But I have no intention of *ever* letting her go.

I fell in love with her as a thirteen-year-old boy. And that love has always been there, always floating right beneath the surface.

Now I have the chance to turn that into something more.

Something that can grow, can mature, can feed us in the years to come.

So no, I don't *have* to do this.

We can be smart, go slow—date and learn each other, fall in love—real, lifelong *adult* love—again. We can play it safe, cautious, move incrementally, step by step by step.

But I've spent my whole life being smart, going step by step.

And that meant I lost Luna when I was a teenager.

It meant I had all these years without her.

I should have kept in touch. I should have told her how deeply I felt back then. I should have done everything I could to keep her in my life.

I didn't.

I fucked up.

So, it may not be smart. It may be wildly out of character for me.

But this is Luns.

She's been my heart since sixth grade.

Ignoring the slowly creeping line, I turn her toward me, cup her jaw, tilting her head up so our gazes align. "Luns," I say again.

"What?" she whispers.

Flowery things flow through my head, big sentiments that I want to declare, but it's too soon for that childhood love and too soon for huge declarations. I need to time to bind her too me, to make her understand, for that love beneath the surface to grow.

Then I realize that's the old me talking.

So...

I embrace the full fuck-it vibe of Vegas and say, "I loved you back then and I let you go."

Her mouth falls open and I take advantage, kissing her deeply, stroking my tongue over hers, tasting her long enough that I hear a cough behind me, that I realize the space in line in front of us has grown to epic proportions.

So, I draw her forward again.

And when we pause again, I bend, murmur in her ear, "That was the biggest mistake of my life, sweetheart."

She sucks in a breath.

"Now, knowing that—" I brush my mouth over hers again, making sure to keep it short and sweet and hot. "So do you honestly think that now that you're back in my life I'm going to ever let you go again?"

TWENTY

Luna

DO *you honestly think that now that you're back in my life I'm going to ever let you go again?*

My hands shake as I do up the zipper on my side.

This is crazy.

And yet, I'm doing up the zipper on a white dress I bought specifically for this moment.

And it's not some frumpy potato sack—it's the prettiest dress I've ever seen. It's something I bought because I imagined what Aiden would think when he saw me, how his face would change and his eyes would warm and his expression would heat.

And now he's waiting just outside the bathroom and I'm seconds away from him seeing it.

Seconds—okay, well, less than an hour—away from marrying him.

What if he doesn't like it? What if I disappoint him?

What if he decides he doesn't want this?

What if—

"Enough," I whisper to myself in the mirror, deliberately shoving the thoughts away, not allowing my brain to go there. I've thought myself into a tizzy the last couple of days. I'm doing this, so what's the point in thinking it to death?

"There isn't a point," I mutter then force out a breath. It's jerky as hell, same as my movements as I put my earrings in, missing the holes more than once before I manage to fasten the backs of the chandelier style adornments.

But I keep breathing.

And I securely fasten the pretty earrings that once belonged to Grams. She had passed them on to my mother, and when Mom died, I inherited them.

So, in a way, it feels like they're both here with me tonight.

I finger the diamond-coated fringe and study myself in the mirror.

The earrings are the only accessory I paired with my dress.

Because the dress is so perfect that I don't need anything else.

It's made of silk that cascades down my body, lightly tracing along my curves, clinging to my breasts, my hips. It gathers slightly near my ankles, highlighting the sparkly, high-heeled sandals whose straps wrap around my calves.

The front is beautiful, understated. Elegant.

The back is sin—dipping down to the top of my ass, the material teasing, calling for a man's fingertips there...then to slip beneath.

And that lingerie I bought, the lacy scraps I intended to wear are in my suitcase.

Because I forgot about the cut of the dress, the lay of the material.

This isn't a dress you wear undergarments with.

No bra straps showing, no underwear lines.

Nope. It's just *me*.

Lace will come...later.

I smooth down the fabric, release another shaking breath. Then there's no point in delaying it.

We have an appointment.

We agreed to do this.

We—

There's a knock at the door.

"Those feet getting chilly, my tiny tornado?"

I glance down at my pink painted toenails, half expecting them to be covered in ice. But they're normal, despite the nerves twining through my middle. Another deep breath, another nibble at the corner of my mouth. Then I slam the door on my worry and focus on what's important.

Making this as good as possible for Aiden.

That thought held tightly to my heart and mind, I reach for the handle and pull open the door.

His gaze locks on mine and I find myself sucking in a breath.

Intense green eyes filled with swirling of emotions that I can barely track—I just know they're big and fierce and...call to that same wealth of feelings inside me.

Then his gaze slips from mine, slowly traveling down the length of my body. It's an almost tangible thing, the heat that travels through me as his eyes trace over me—my breasts, my torso, my waist, my hips. My thighs tremble when he reaches my ankles, my shoes and his mouth curves up.

"Like the heels, sweetheart."

It's a soft rumble that slides through me, tracing between my legs, flicking over my clit.

I exhale shakily. "Do you like the dress too?"

His mouth curves further.

Then he reaches forward, snagging my hand, drawing it

back toward his body the same time as he steps forward, closing the distance between us. "Do you feel that?" he asks, settling it on his cock.

His *hard* cock.

My fingers tighten and he groans softly.

"You like it," I murmur.

"Yeah, Luns." He gently peels my hand free, presses a kiss to my palm. "I like it." A beat. "Too fucking much."

I lift on tiptoe, brush my lips over his. "There's no such thing."

"It is if I drag you over to the bed, strip you naked, and show you how much I like the dress and heels."

Heat blooms through my middle, shoots out through my limbs.

"Don't look like that, tiny tornado."

"Like what?"

"Like you want me to do just that."

"I do," I say, giggling softly when he groans. Then, just because I'm a glutton for punishment and maybe also because I really *really* like it that he wants me so badly and isn't shy about showing it, I lift on tiptoe again and murmur in his ear, "I'm not wearing any underwear."

He groans again, hands clamping onto my hips, my name on his lips. "Behave," he mutters a moment later. "Until later," he adds, bending and stealing a kiss that leaves me breathless.

When I come back down to earth, he's staring at my breasts and I realize my nipples are beaded, pressing against the thin material.

"No underwear," he says approvingly.

And...I laugh.

Because I'm no longer worried or upset or feeling lonely.

And maybe also because, *God*, I really like this man.

Especially when he takes my hand, starts drawing us to the door. "Let's go get married, my tiny tornado."

"AND NOW, by the power vested in me by the State of Nevada, I now pronounce you husband and wife..."

My lungs spasm.

My fingers tighten around Aiden's.

My eyes lock onto his, the emotions inside me reflected in the emerald depths of his gaze.

Because this moment is big, important, beautiful—

At least until Elvis says, "You may kiss your hunka, hunka burning love."

Then my lips twitch and I know that Aiden is feeling the same curl of amusement as I am. Hunka, hunka burning love? Ha. That's so perfectly *Vegas,* it's not even funny. Or it is. Whatever. Frankly, with all the big emotions I've been feeling, I'm just thankful for the humor, for Aiden to be choking back laughter too while standing across the altar from me.

Reciting the vows to love and cherish, in sickness and in health, till death do us part was intense.

Real.

Especially while staring into those emerald eyes of his, seeing that he was feeling the words just as deeply as I was.

This is usually an ending, the happily ever after for couples.

But, for Aiden and me, it feels like the beginning.

And that feels...important, heavy, serious.

Elvis telling me to kiss my hunka, hunka burning love?

Not so much.

Elvis clears his throat and smiling, I close the distance between Aiden's and my bodies, pressing myself against his front, feeling the hard length of his body, the strong embrace of his arms. I'm surrounded by the spicy scent of him, am lost in all the sensations of the boy I loved, the man I'm learning...and yet still somehow know.

Which is why it feels like the most natural thing in the word to lean up and kiss him.

Elvis and all his rhinestones disappear.

The music and the witnesses we hired fade to the background.

I'm not feeling the slight chill in the air, the pinch of my shoes.

I'm not worried that I'm taking advantage of Aiden, that I'm going to mess up his life, that we're somehow going to have to explain this to his family...and deal with the fallout of mine.

It's just Aiden and me.

And this one beautiful moment.

That feels like a beginning.

TWENTY-ONE

Aiden

"OH, GOD!" she screams, her head dropping back against the headboard, her hips grinding hard against my mouth.

Her dress is rucked up around her waist, and I have her spread wide, her legs pinned to the bed, that gorgeous pussy on display as I fuck her with my mouth and fingers and tongue.

Beautiful.

Sexy.

Mine.

"Oh my fucking God!" she screams.

And I feel it—the slickness increasing, her body shuddering, my name tumbling off her lips as she comes apart.

She goes limp, her moan cascading through the air, eyes sliding closed.

And I can't take it any longer, can't hold back.

I've made her come with my fingers, then with my mouth, then with my fingers *and* my mouth, and now my dick is about to break in half.

I reach for the box of condoms, tearing it open, pulling one out.

A half second later, I'm rolling it down the length of my cock, positioning myself at her entrance. I know I should go slow. I know I should go easy. But my control is fucked, so I thrust home.

Her eyes fly open on a gasp.

"Too much?" I grunt.

"No," she moans, hips lifting to meet mine as I stroke deep. "It's good, Aiden. God, *that's* good. Don't stop, I—"

I can't stop.

Probably couldn't even if my life depended on it.

That sexy as sin dress that caresses every inch of her gorgeous body crumpled up around her waist, yanked down to expose plump, delicious breasts.

Those heels that sparkled and teased and now are currently digging into my back as I fuck her hard and fast.

Naked flesh that goes pink and slick.

Gray eyes that are shot full of lightning as she comes on my tongue.

And now...on my cock.

She convulses around me, pussy clamping so hard my eyes roll back. "That's it, sweetheart," I groan as my own orgasm rises up and sucks me under, yanking me beneath the current, sending my own strokes wild. I lose all rhythm, all control.

But it's okay.

Because she's lost in her pleasure too.

"Aiden!" she cries as my vision goes black, my limbs go heavy, and then I'm fucking decimated by my orgasm, torn down to the bones and built back up again, piece by piece by *piece*. By the time I manage to open my eyes, to descend back to Earth, it's to find that I've collapsed on top of Luna.

"Shit," I mutter, realizing I'm probably crushing her and lifting up, rolling us to our sides.

I lose her, my dick sliding free of the slick, tight clasp of her pussy.

"I liked it," she murmurs, arms looping around my shoulders, her leg hitching around my waist. "The weight of you." She nuzzles at my throat, lips pressing lightly to my skin.

"Good," I say, smoothing my hand down her back. "Because I don't think I could have moved anyway."

She giggles softly, shoves a strand of hair out of her face.

I snag her hand, kiss her knuckles. "You like it?" I ask about the ring I bought her.

Shy eyes. Pink cheeks. Her fingers closing around mine. "It's too much."

"No, it's not."

I mean, should I have gone as all out as I had for a ring for a marriage that's essentially a business agreement?

Probably not.

But it's Luna.

It's Luna and me.

And Smythe stocks and Grams's interference or not, Luna is mine.

So the ring is going to reflect that.

"If it's not your style," I murmur, lightly running my finger over the smooth metal band, "the jeweler said we could exchange it for something else."

"It's beautiful," she says, holding tight to my hand. "More than I could have ever imagined."

I kiss her nose. "Good."

She exhales, nuzzles against my throat again, body relaxing against mine. "Now what?"

"Room service," I say. "As soon as I summon the energy to

pick up the phone. Food and more champagne and then"—I nip at her ear—"more eating you out."

She shivers, arching against me. "I like this plan."

"Mmm," I say, the curves of her awakening my still hard dick. God, I feel eighteen again, like I can go all night without a break, can fuck her over and over again. "Or," I murmur, "we could delay the room service and champagne and I can go straight back to licking that delicious pussy of yours."

Another shiver.

And, grinning wolfishly, I realize she's given her answer.

"I'll take care of the condom." A kiss to the spot behind her ear. "You just lay there and think of all the ways I'm going to fuck you."

"*Aiden.*"

I steal her lips in a drugging kiss then force myself up and out of bed, going into the bathroom and disposing of the condom. I grab the open bottle of champagne—because I have ideas for that too, namely lick it off her naked body.

I set it on the nightstand, crawl back into bed beside her, pausing to undo her shoes and slide them free before kissing my way up her legs.

I'm just reaching for the bottle again when there's a knock at the door.

"Ignore it," she murmurs when I freeze with my mouth about an inch from that plump wet pussy.

Nodding, I make that inch disappear, sliding my tongue through her.

She moans, hips bucking, head dropping back to the pillows.

And there's another fucking knock.

Fuck.

I push it out of my mind. They have the wrong door, the wrong floor, the wrong fucking *room*.

KNOCK! KNOCK! KNOCK!

Luna jerks, head flying up. "Wh—?"

"Goddamn it." I launch myself out of bed, yank the blankets up and over her, then stomp away from the bed, temper ratcheting higher and higher with every step.

Mostly because the knocking keeps coming as I snag a towel, wrap it around my waist.

And doesn't stop as I reach for the handle.

Nor when I growl as I whip open the door...

To find Smitty standing in the hall.

"Happy Belated Birthday motherfucker!" he shouts.

And then he barges right past me.

TWENTY-TWO

Luna

WHY ARE people always bursting into the bedroom when I'm naked?

I clutch the blankets to my chin as a huge, bearded man barrels his way into the room. Then stops, mouth dropping open.

"Christ," Aiden says, shoving past him then standing in front of the bigger man, doing his best to block me from view. "You being at a loss for words would be funny," he mutters, "if only you weren't in my fucking hotel room."

The door to said room slams closed, making me jump and seeming to jar the big man.

He looks around Aiden and waves at me, a boyish smile curving his mouth. "Um...sorry to intrude," he says, his voice just as big as his body—and beard. "I'll just hit the door and let you two get back to...your *fun* time." He hitches a thumb over his shoulder and starts to turn, spinning away from the bed, rotating toward the dresser.

Then stopping, shock ricocheting through his form.

"A marriage license?" he asks, turning back toward us, his mouth falling open a second time.

Which is when Aiden's had enough.

He plunks a hand onto the big man's chest, shoves him toward the door, sending him staggering back several steps. "Really, Smitty. It's time for you to get the fuck out."

The aforementioned Smitty brushes Aiden's hand off like it's a feather then lurches forward, grabbing the signed and notarized paper. "It *is* a fucking marriage license! Holy shit, dude!" His grin is nearly as big as the rest of him. "You're fucking married? To the hottie from the pictures your mom sent? Do your parents know?" He leans in, lowers his voice—which is to say, the volume of his words decreases, but he's still loud as hell. "Are you sure this is wise? Vegas, buddy, it can be the land of magic...but also of regrets." A beat. "Do you...like... really"—his eyes slide toward me, chagrin in the deep brown depths, and voice drops further, as if he's just realizing I can hear every word—"*know* her?"

I bite my lip, stifling a giggle.

If Smitty only knew.

But Aiden isn't amused. He groans, eyes closing, and I can practically see him counting to ten—then twenty when patience doesn't come after the first interval.

"Um," I say, drawing the big man's focus again. "Aiden and I grew up together. So yeah," I finish. "We know each other pretty well."

His brown eyes come to mine, and he takes a step toward me, though I don't miss that he stops immediately when I clutch the blankets a little tighter to my chest. "I'm Smitty," he says, voice going gentle.

"Luna," I reply softly. "Maybelle."

"Nice to meet you, Luna Maybelle," he says, still in that

gentle voice, then looks away, giving me at least a blip of privacy.

"Great," Aiden mutters. "Now that introductions have been made all around, you"—he glares at Smitty—"can get the fuck out."

"Hell no, man!" Smitty says. "We're in Vegas. You're married to a beautiful woman who seems nice"—another slanting glance of deep brown eyes and the mischief in them has me wanting to giggle again—"we've got to celebrate!"

"There is absolutely no *we* where you're involved, Smitty," Aiden grits out, every word sounding like he's gargling broken glass. "*Luna and I* are going to celebrate. You're going to go back the fuck to your hotel room and leave us alone."

Smitty pouts.

It's a ridiculous expression on a grown man, not the least of which one of Smitty's size.

But it's also somehow...cute?

I like him.

"But you didn't even tell us so we could throw you a party," he grumbles. "And you know I throw a great party."

Aiden shoves a hand through his hair. "We *eloped* Smitty. That means we kept it a secret from everyone so we could enjoy things like *our wedding night* in private."

Smitty's pout deepens.

Aiden sighs and tilts his head back, staring at the ceiling for a moment. "Look," he says, dropping his head back down. "My mom is going to freak out and likely throw something together the moment she finds out. You leave us alone until we get back to the Bay Area and I'll make sure you get an invite."

The big man considers that for a long, *long* moment.

"Don't push me, Smitty," Aiden mutters.

"It'd be better if we plan it together—your mom and I," Smitty says contritely, while not *looking* contrite in the least.

"That's not going to happen." Aiden glares. "And if you push it, I'll make sure the theme is wombats."

I don't really understand what that means, but Smitty does, apparently. He shudders. "That's not fair," he says begrudgingly. "But fine."

"*Wombats*," Aiden repeats. "With beady little black eyes and cube-shaped poop."

Smitty pales slightly and shives. "Ugh. Like I said, *fine*. But"—he jabs a finger in Aiden's direction—"the party better be soon. And if your mom reaches out because she wants my help then I'm telling you've okayed it."

Why am I almost certain that Kathy Black is going to *reach out* to Smitty for party planning help?

I keep that thought to myself, along with the guilt that threatens to rise up about Kathy planning a party for a business deal of a marriage.

This isn't purely that.

I know it. Aiden knows it.

And anyway, I can flagellate myself later.

Tonight, I just want to enjoy Aiden...and maybe also the big man's shenanigan's. So long as he leaves soon.

"Dude," Aiden mutters, shoving at his chest again. "Just get the fuck out of here."

Likely realizing that he's pushed Aiden to a breaking point, Smitty finally cooperates, letting himself be herded toward and out the door, calling a goodbye to me in the process.

I call one back, thinking—yeah, I can't help it—but I like the man.

I hear the heavy wooden panel slam closed. Then a *thunk*, like Aiden's dropping his head against it.

Carefully, I get out of bed, peeling off my bunched up dress and hanging it over the back of the chair. I take a step toward the door then pause...debating.

Yeah. The aftermath of Smitty's interruption definitely calls for lacy undergarments.

So, I change directions, snagging the lingerie from my bag. It takes only a couple of seconds to clip on the bra, to drag the matching panties up my thighs.

And when Aiden doesn't reappear in that time, I venture down the short hall, see that he's got his face pressed to the door.

He sighs loudly.

Smiling despite myself, I settle my hand on his back. "Wombats?"

He spins beneath my touch, emerald eyes filled with irritation. "You don't want to know."

"I do," I say. "Like, I *really* do."

Smitty seems incorrigible enough that I'll need ammunition for future interactions.

"No, you don't..." But he trails off, eyes heating as his gaze drags down my front, catching on my breasts, dipping lower to the scrap of fabric that is masquerading as underwear. "*Luns.*"

I shiver, heat gathering between my legs, making the tops of my thighs slick with need. "You like?"

"As much as that dress and those heels?" He shakes his head. "No. *Fuck* no."

One side of my mouth curves up.

Especially when he adds, "But is it a close second? Oh yeah, sweetheart."

"I—"

But I don't even know what I would have said next because whatever bit of sass had risen up in my throat, preparing to escape and tease this man who I desperately want to be mine is cut off when he wraps an arm around my middle and drags me against him, lips sealing over mine, tongue sliding into my mouth.

He kisses me long and deep and wet.

And even before he gives me a moment to catch my breath, before he scoops me up and carries me to the bed...

I'm ready.

He isn't, though.

He takes his time stripping the lacy undergarments from my body as he kisses me, as he strokes and licks and touches, as he caresses and worships and loves, as he guides me up and sends me over the edge before coaxing me back down.

Only, just as he rolls on another condom and starts to stroke home...

There's another knock at the door.

One that doesn't stop.

One that means I'm clutching the blankets to my chin and Aiden is cursing up a blue streak again.

One that means he's pulling away from me and answering the door in a towel, also again.

Thank God for small miracles, it's not another hockey player intruding.

Though, the interruption *is* from Smitty—at least according to the note on the room service tray, tucked between the plates of food, it's corner secured beneath the bottle of champagne.

To keep your energy up.

-S

P.S. It had better be a really good party.

TWENTY-THREE

Aiden

I SNAG my gas station hot dog from the snack table, along with a can of Coke.

There was no morning skate for the team today—something I was very thankful for when I crawled my ass out of the hotel room's bed this afternoon.

Yup.

This *afternoon*.

Because Luns and I spent all night and all day in bed. Fucking and laughing, talking and kissing. Eating room service and going through all the towels in the room because we had to get cleaned up...and then I needed to make sure every inch of her was soaped and stroked and scrubbed to perfection.

The best day.

Starting with that beautiful dress. Then the vows, the kiss, the fact that she became mine. Scorching the sheets. Learning the small intricacies of her again and some I never knew—like how she smiles in her sleep and wants to be held close as she drifts off to sleep. Remembering the way her cheeks go pink as I tease her and her absolute obsession with watching cooking shows on the Food Network.

Little pieces of her.

And I'm soaking them up.

Because it's like the last eighteen hours of perfection have existed on a distant planet, just the two of us—

Smitty's interruptions.

Okay, not *just* the two of us.

But luckily, the room service intrusion he orchestrated was much better than him actually showing up with a bottle of champagne.

And it was nice, I guess, sending fuel over so I could continue pleasuring my woman until she completely passed out.

But it was still annoying.

Because it's Smitty.

And now I'm going to have to thank him for the gesture.

Ugh.

But as I'm eating my hot dog and drinking my Coke, I'm already back to smiling, to feeling like I'm a hundred feet tall.

Because I left Luns passed out in bed—as in, *passed out.*

So much so that I paid for the room for an extra day and she promised to rest until she my game tonight. She'll watch me play and then catch a ride to the airport afterward.

I wish I could go back with her, but we have two more stops on this road trip—Utah and Denver.

Then the team will be home for a bit and all will be good.

Or as good as it can be with me returning with a wife my family doesn't know about and Smitty acting like a dog to a bone wanting to help plan us a party to celebrate.

But that's a problem for another day.

I'll break it to my parents—suggest the party...and fucking Smitty as necessary.

Right now, I need to suck back my soda, start in on my dog, and hope that the combination will give my tired ass body enough energy to play well.

Can't stink it up in front of my wife.

Grinning, I polish off the Coke, toss the empty can in the recycle bin, then feeling the caffeine beginning to hit my blood stream, I reach for another.

Not exactly on the nutrition guidelines, but desperate needs, desperate measures and all that.

Suitably full of sugar after the second can, I turn for the locker room.

"I wouldn't go in there," I hear.

Freezing, I glance over my shoulder, not having noticed my teammate—what with my marital bliss and all that. Gray's wearing one of his fancy, expensive suits and is leaning, arms and ankles crossed, back against the opposite wall from me. "Yeah?" I ask tentatively. "Why not?"

Gray studies me for a long moment.

Then sighs and shakes his head.

Yeah, I don't like that. Not at all.

"Smitty's got a bug in his ass," Gray says. "He's put streamers and shit up in all the lockers and your stall is currently full of confetti."

My fingers squeeze on my hot dog, ketchup coating my fingers.

The fucker.

For the confetti *and* making me smoosh my dog.

"I'm going to kill him," I grumble.

Gray almost smiles and if I weren't so annoyed with Smitty,

I would file that away for the history books since it happens so infrequently. "Don't worry," he assures me. "I've called in the reinforcements."

My brows drag together.

But then my expression clears.

Because *then* my teammate Ryan comes around the corner, his arms full of the one thing that can tame the big, bearded beast currently making trouble in the locker room.

"Jesus," Gray mutters. "You couldn't find a bigger one?"

"This is Vegas." Ryan shoves the giant stuffed toy at Gray. "You know they don't do things small."

"That's Texas, dumbass." Gray shoves it back. "Everything's bigger in Texas."

Ryan rolls his eyes. "Fine. How about Vegas doesn't do anything in half measures?"

"Less catchy," Gray mutters. "More accurate."

Ryan shakes his head, drops the huge stuffed animal on the table. "Either way, I did you the favor. Now I need to get ready for the game."

"You're the only guy on the team who was making a pit stop at the toy store."

Ryan narrows his eyes, tucks the arm with the other bag I'd previously missed a bit further behind his back. "How'd you know that?" It's a frosty question.

One that doesn't bother Gray in the least. "Alex's birthday is the day we get back, right?"

Alex? Oh, *Alex*.

Right.

My brows go up, impressed that my captain has his finger on the pulse of my teammate that closely, and think—perhaps for the first time ever—that Smitty might be on to something with all his nosiness. Mostly because Ryan has the hots for a single mom named Veronica...who's friend-zoned him with complete and utter certainty.

And that seems complicated.

And interesting.

And maybe...like we can do something to help him out of the friend zone.

"I'm getting dressed," Ryan growls, not acknowledging Gray's question as he brushes by us.

"Please don't accept any confetti from Smitty," I say—or maybe beg.

Ryan pauses, his mouth twitching, just the slightest bit, but he doesn't comment further. He only claps me on the arm and pushes into the locker room.

Great.

He's so going to get in on the confetti action too.

And God, I love Smitty—the man's heart is as big as his body.

But sometimes—or maybe *most* of the time—I really want to throttle him.

"Finish your hot dog. Down that sugar." Gray nods to my snacks. "Then take all the time you need to get your head in the game. But"—he jerks his head at the table covered mostly by the stuffed brown-fuzzed marsupial—"when you come into the locker room, make sure you do it wielding wombats."

THE WOMBAT WORKS and I manage to only find a few stray pieces of paper in my jock after the game.

I have no clue why Smitty is scared of the adorably cuddly creatures, but he is.

And considering how much of a handful he is, I'm just glad to have a way to kind of, sort of control him.

Off the ice, anyway.

On the ice, he's as much of a beast as always—skating hard, shooting hard, passing...you guessed it, *hard*.

And we need it against the Rattlers.

The bite as viciously as the actual reptile, never out of striking range, no matter how big of a lead we have.

Tonight, they almost sneak back in and strike like their namesake.

Luckily, I'm fueled by Coke and hot dog and the night of orgasms.

And that helps me see the breakaway developing the wrong fucking way—that being *toward* our goalie instead of to the goal we're trying to score on—before the Rattlers actually send the puck sailing down the ice.

So I'm already hauling ass back, skating hard for our zone when I hear—

Crack!

Glancing up, I watch the puck fly through the neutral zone, see it land on the Rattlers' player's stick.

Even though it's not an easy pass to corral, Kit St. James doesn't miss a beat, using his speed to his advantage and quickly getting behind our defense.

I'm ready, though.

I'm sprinting, tearing down the ice, cutting between him and our goalie—

Right as he winds up for a slap shot.

Fuck.

I brace, turning my head away, knowing there's no stopping myself now, no getting the fuck out of the way and letting the guy with the specialized pads—our fucking goalie—be the one to stop the wicked fast shot.

Nope.

This is all me.

Another *crack!*

I have a split second to watch out of the corner of my eye, to watch the puck fly toward me, to know this is going to really fucking *hurt.*

And then...

The world goes black.

TWENTY-FOUR

Luna

"I NEED TO SEE AIDEN!" I tell the security guard. "Aiden Black from the Grizzlies."

He looks down his nose at me.

Probably because I'm acting like a crazed fan.

When really, I'm a panicked wife.

Then, not deigning to answer, he looks away, going back to his job of manning the hallway and not allowing any peons like me back into the player's area.

"It's just. He got hurt and..." I bite my lip, force the words out. "He's my husband." His brows lift, but he doesn't otherwise comment. "I tried calling him, but he didn't pick up."

Probably because he was stretchered off the ice.

My husband of one day—

My friend.

The boy I loved.

The man who welcomed me back with open arms.

And we've had one day together before my bad luck, before the Maybelle curse, has infiltrated his life.

That's nonsense, baby girl. I hear Gram's voice in my head. *The curse isn't real and you know it.*

I *don't* know it.

Because my mom, my sister, Grams, and now...the man I care about.

No, it's more than that. More than caring.

Aiden is...the man I never stopped loving.

And this is my fault. My fault. *My—*

"Hey!" I hear and my gaze jerks from the big, hulking man in front of me to the big, hulking man striding my way.

Smitty's hair is sweaty and he's still half-dressed, but his eyes are calm and collected as they hold mine. "He's good," is the first thing he says when he gets close enough to speak at a semi-normal—but what I assume is quiet for him—volume. "They're taking him over to the hospital for a CT—"

I gasp.

He just reaches forward, his big hand surrounding mine as he holds my fingers securely. "That's a normal thing, babe. They follow the concussion protocol after a shot to the head like that."

"They stretchered him off," I push out between numb lips.

God, I hate watching him play hockey.

"Yeah, they did." He tugs me toward him, saying to the security guard, "She's with us, yeah?"

The guard nods back, steps aside to let me pass.

But I barely notice.

Because I'm too focused on Smitty and what he's saying. "Aiden was alert and talking when they brought him back. He's with the trainer now and you can go to the hospital with him if you want."

"Does he—?" I pause, nibble at my lip again.

"Does he what?" It's a gentle question, far gentler than anything I've heard from him up to this point, and I find that the soft tone means that I can push out the rest of the very scary questions.

"Does he want me there, you think?"

Something crosses behind Smitty's eyes.

Then he tucks a wayward strand of my hair behind my ear. "Yeah, honey," he says quietly. "He wants you there."

I nod, and when he tucks me close to his side, I barely even notice that he's sweaty, that he doesn't smell all that great. I'm just thankful for his size and strength and guidance as he takes me through the twisting corridors without hesitation.

It's only when we stop outside a closed door that the nerves start to come back.

"He's fine," Smitty says, seeing me hesitate. "He's with Doc, but you can go in."

I nod again.

Smitty knocks and we hear a voice call out to, "Come in!"

"You got this." Smitty smiles encouragingly as he twists the door handle, pushes the wooden panel inward.

I start to step inside then stop, turn back. "Smitty?"

His gentle giant gaze comes to mine. "Yeah, Luna girl?"

My heart pulses at the nickname, but I don't have space to process how nice that feels, how nice he's being, how much I like all of that, how much I want it to be forever, to have men like him, a man like Aiden in my life.

But I don't have time to verbalize all of that.

So, I just nod at Smitty and murmur, "Thanks."

Somehow, I think he sees all of that flowing through my head because he nods, mouth kicking up on one side. "You're welcome."

Then he strolls away, skates clomping on the mats as he walks.

I shore up my courage, brace against what I might see, then move into the room.

And go completely still.

Aiden is watching me, his green eyes lucid and clear.

"Oh, my God!" I gasp that panic lurching to life again. "Are you okay?"

His eyes might be lucid and clear but there's a bruise blooming on his cheek. A huge, ugly bruise with—

"Oh, my God," I gasp again.

Of course he's not okay.

He got hit with a puck in the freaking head!

"Luns," he says.

And there are stitches in his cheek, a neat line of them bisecting all of that black and blue and purple.

"*Luns,*" he says again.

I blink.

Realize that he's holding his hand out. "Come here, sweetheart."

Only, my feet can't move. They're glued to the floor and something trails through his expression when he seems to realize that. "Am I good?"

My eyebrows drag together because that doesn't make sense.

He's not good—he has a honking bruise on his face and stitches holding his skin together and he got hit in the freaking head with a freaking puck and—

"You're good," I hear the other man say—the one who must be the team's doctor, or *Doc* as Smitty referred to him.

Doctor or not, I open my mouth to remind them both that Aiden is *not* good.

But before I get that out, he's on his feet and moving toward me.

I notice that his gait is smooth, even, that his eyes continue to remain lucid and pain free, but it's only when his fingers wrap around mine and he pulls me against his chest that I manage to speak. "You're not good," I fret, running my free hand gently over his chest and arms and shoulders, not daring to touch him anywhere near those bruises or the cut that's been sewn closed. "You need to sit down and—"

The other man brushes by me with a soft, "Excuse me."

"Thanks, Doc," Aiden says over my head.

"Any time." A beat. "Meet in the parking lot when you're ready and we'll get the scan taken care of, yeah?"

"Yeah, Doc."

The door closes and I push back gently against his chest, accuse, "You're hurt."

"It's only five stitches," he says and I feel my mouth fall open.

"Only *five* stitches? That's five too many! Not to mention the bruise and the fact that you were carried off the ice on a stretcher!"

My voice catches and I clamp my lips together.

His eyes twinkle. "You're trying to not to demand that I quit hockey, aren't you?"

The question is amused, but I'm anything but.

Because I was thinking *exactly* that.

And it's annoying he knows that.

Because it's not rational and because I can't help but think exactly that and because he has five *freaking* stitches in his face.

"We need to get you to the hospital."

"The CT is just a precaution."

"Smitty said it's part of the concussion protocol."

He scowls. "Smitty is a fucking loudmouth."

I take his hand, draw him forward. "We need to get your stuff."

He shrugs and shakes his head. "The team will grab it and

make sure it's on the plane." He slips his hand from mine, goes back to the table where he'd been sitting, where he'd been sitting getting those fucking *stitches*. "And your bag is here."

I frown.

He answers the unspoken question, "I sent someone back to the hotel to get it."

Because I couldn't bring it into the arena, so I'd left it with the concierge.

"Aiden," I whisper, heart squeezing.

"You're not alone anymore, Luns."

My heart squeezes again.

"And we have each other's backs, right?" He touches my cheek. "You worrying about me and a few stitches and I..." His lips brush over my forehead. "And *I* need to...make sure that sexy lingerie makes its way back home."

TWENTY-FIVE

Aiden

LUNA and her sexy lingerie make it back home days before I do.

But that was always the plan—Luna needed to get back to her job at the non-profit, and she needed to speak with her attorney, get the ball rolling on the shares of Smythe before time runs out.

And not that it's a surprise to me or Doc, but my CT turns out fine, and I clear the concussion protocol without issue.

Which means I play against Denver *and* Utah—of course, I do it wearing a full cage which is annoying because while it protects those puny five stitches, it also blocks my vision and makes me feel like that youth hockey player who first fell for Luna all those years before.

Luna.

Who worried about me in adorable fashion, calling to check on me more often than my mom, texting and FaceTiming and just genuinely...*worrying*.

Honestly, if it was any other woman, I would have lost my shit and told her to back off.

This is my job—blood and bruises, stitches and broken bones, they're all par for the course.

But...it was Luns calling me.

Her worry touches and amuses me in equal measure.

I'll be happy when the stitches are out, though.

Because even through FaceTime her gaze catches on my injury, those gray eyes clouding over.

She had quite a welcome to having a professional hockey-playing husband.

Blood and a hospital visit barely twenty-four hours after tying the knot is a lot.

Poor thing.

I'll have to make it up to her with orgasms.

Mouth kicking up, I toss my bag over my shoulder, then follow my teammates off the bus. The Grizzlies' plane is parked all of forty feet away and I hurry across the tarmac, the autumn wind whipping through my clothing, slicing against my skin.

Damn.

Too much time in California means that my blood has thinned again.

Before I know it, I'll be thinking that sixty degrees is cold.

"Damn, man, that expression looks good on you."

I jerk, realize that Smitty is watching me over his shoulder, beard twitching. "What nonsense are you talking now?"

He clamps a hand to his chest. "I send you gifts, celebrate your milestones, and this is the gift I get in return?"

I just glower at him, keep walking.

"Just saying," he booms. "Happily fucking married looks good on you."

Sighing, I glance back at him over my shoulder. "I'm going

to sic Kailey on you," I say of his wife, who may appear quiet and shy, but has a stubborn streak a mile wide. "She won't like that you're giving me a hard time."

"Nice try, A-man," Smitty says as he starts pounding up the stairs beside me. "I filled her in, and she's just as curious as I am about your Luna—especially since she seems to have come out of nowhere."

I follow him onto the plane. "I told you—"

"That you and Luna were childhood sweethearts until you broke. Yeah, yeah all that's great." He turns down the aisle. "But there's more to the story. I can feel it in my bones."

God, the man is just fucking—

"Give it a rest, Smitty, yeah?" Gray says, coming up behind us. "It's late. We're all ready to be home. Interrogate Aiden another time."

Smitty sinks down in his seat with a scowl, and I take advantage of his momentary distraction to take a different spot a few rows back.

But my teammate...well, he isn't one to let go of a thread of gossip.

Hasn't ever been.

Won't start tonight.

He just lets Gray pass then stands, spinning to face me, resting his arms on the top of the seat, his eyes locking onto mine as he says, "I'll get to the bottom of this, A-man. I always do."

"Great," I mutter. "Threats."

"Cool it, Smitty," Ryan says, sinking down beside me. "Or I'll tell Aiden which store I visited in Vegas."

For a second, I frown, not getting it.

Then I do.

The wombat.

The only thing that seems to keep Smitty in check.

And, thankfully, it works for me today too.

He shudders and turns back around, dropping into his chair.

I exhale. Ryan bumps his shoulder against mine. "It'll pass."

"Says who?" I grumble.

"Says the man who's in his crosshairs."

I lift my brows in question.

"Since Smitty's focused on the rest of us"—Ryan makes air quotes—"single fuckers."

There is that.

If I'm off the market, I should eventually be off his radar.

"That's actually a really good point." I bump *his* shoulder this time. "But in the meantime, maybe I should remind him again that *you're* single. Get some of the heat off me."

Ryan's meets my gaze, challenge written all over his expression. "You do that and I'll join him in figuring out why this Luna of yours has appeared seemingly out of nowhere, after you not mentioning her"—his lifts his eyebrows—"*ever* and now you're suddenly married."

Fuck.

"It's complicated."

"No shit," he deadpans, but then his mouth curves the slightest bit. "Is she as gorgeous as Smitty says?"

"Even more so," I tell him. "He only saw the outside package that is my Luns. He didn't even get to see the beauty she has inside her."

Ryan's expression clears, going completely blank for one long second.

The next, he's back to the Ryan I've learned over the last months—quiet and slightly removed from the rest of us, but so easily slipping under the radar that it's hard to catch a glimpse of the storm he's hiding beneath that calm, unconcerned exterior.

Or so I've thought.

Because tonight he gives me more than a glimpse.

Tonight, his quiet words reach my ears just as the fasten seatbelt sign dings on overhead.

"If you find a woman who lets you in deep enough to see the beauty inside her, to know the soft underbelly of her, to understand the puzzle pieces that make up the bigger picture of her soul..." He sighs, yanks his headphones out of his bag. "Don't let that go—no matter how hard she tries to push you away."

"I—"

But he doesn't give me any more than that.

Just puts in his earbuds and closes his eyes.

Leaving me to know...he's unequivocally right.

Which is why I have no plans of letting Luna go.

TWENTY-SIX

Luna

I CLOSE the spreadsheet I've been working on—an inventory of the donations the shelter received over the last two weeks—and stretch.

My eyes are bleary and my shoulders ache from being at the computer.

But the inventory is complete and now we can figure out what we need to order to flesh out the rest of our supplies.

The non-profit I work at is part shelter, part food pantry, part job training.

We function mostly on the backs of our volunteers, aside from a skeletal staff of psychologists, social workers, and...our graduates—those who've moved from seeking aid to providing it.

It's great—*really* great actually.

The non-profit pays for most of its expenses through a cafe that's partnered with Molly's Bakery, a longtime staple here in the Bay. And our girls who go into that program learn everything from washing dishes to ordering inventory to running a cash register to making a business plan for their future endeavors.

We have something for everyone.

And all the profits—after payroll, because the girls need money to start a life after the shelter—go right back in to funding the shelter and its programs.

It's going so well, in fact, that we're getting ready to open another location—*if* we can get the fundraising in line.

That's a problem for another day, though.

It's late, so much later than I normally ever stay here at work, but I wanted to clear the decks.

Because Aiden has tomorrow off.

And we're going to share "our surprise" with his family.

So, even *if* Aiden was already back from his road trip and I was in bed with him, I likely wouldn't be sleeping anyway.

Before I showed up on his doorstep, it had been more than a decade since I saw him and his family.

Then I barely blinked before I was naked in his bed, before his family was there hauling me along to breakfast and the game...something I ruined because I panicked and ran away, making a scene, making it about me, making a terrible first impression the second time over—

Now we're going to announce that we're *married?*

God, there's no way I'll sleep tonight.

The thought of disappointing Kathy and Matt, Carrie and Ralph and Dave...of disappointing Aiden...

My stomach is in knots.

"Enough," I whisper.

But it's not that easy to shove the emotions down. Even when I try to remind myself that Aiden is doing me a favor, that this isn't that serious.

Do you honestly think that now that you're back in my life I'm going to ever let you go again?

Right. Not serious. *Sure.*

Groaning, I slam the door on my swirling thoughts and vow that I'm not going to make things more complicated for him.

We're...friends.

Who give each other lots of orgasms.

And who get married so I can fulfill my crazy grandmother's edict on my quest to try and do something good in this world.

Simple, right?

Sighing, I sit back in my chair, my hands resting lightly on my middle, the ring Aiden bought me glittering on my left hand. I turn it from side to side, watching it sparkle in the overhead lights, and sigh again.

Because I know what Aiden's giving *me*...

But again...what am I going to give him that's even remotely worthy in return?

Orgasms only go so far, and it's not like I bring much to the table aside from drama and complications. God knows that even my family slots into those categories— what with Gram's will and my dad and brother being their usual vindictive selves.

It's only going to get worse too.

Because once they find out that the shares are going to be mine, they're going to get nasty. And then it won't just be showing up and demanding I come to board meetings, it will be attacks and lawyers and incursions at all hours of the day and night as they try to get me to back down.

"But that's not tonight," I whisper, dropping my hands to the desk. A few taps on my keyboard and clicks of the mouse has my file saved and my computer shutting down and then I'm snagging my purse from the bottom drawer.

The way I see it, I have two big issues—my brother and

father, and the fact that I have no way to pay Aiden back for marrying me.

I don't even really know who he is anymore—outside of the big stuff that is.

I know he's kind and good and prefers vanilla cake and frosting over the plethora of other delicious options there are out there. I know he loves his family and cares for his friends and will always go the distance for them.

Case in point?

Me.

But what are the small things that make him tick? What wishes does he hold dear, hoping they'll work out some day? Does he want a dog? A cat? A hamster? Where does he want to travel? Or is he sick of all the plane rides and bus trips and would prefer to have a staycation instead?

Is a grilled peanut butter and jelly sandwich still his favorite meal? Or has his palate grown and changed and he likes something like blinis with beluga caviar?

I snort because I think that no matter how many years have passed, Aiden will never be the type of man who prefers caviar over white bread and Jif peanut butter and Smucker's strawberry jelly.

Nostalgia reigns supreme.

The past is important to him.

It doesn't rule his present, but it certainly impacts his future—it's in the pictures on his walls and the memories he's shared, and...the way he opened his home and heart and ring finger to me.

I toss my purse over my shoulder, shove back my chair, and move to the door, flicking out the lights to my office.

It's those thoughts that are running through my mind as I wave goodbye to our security guard—more volunteers, these being off-duty police officers who take turns keeping an eye on things to ensure those seeking shelter here are protected.

And it's those thoughts that ping through my brain as I unlock my car, climb inside, and then start the ignition.

But it's those thoughts that coalesce into crystal clear clarity as I drive home.

Because I know *exactly* how to make sure I'm not just blindly accepting Aiden's help.

I know at least one small thing that he'll love.

TWENTY-SEVEN

Aiden

I'M NOT GOING to lie—I'm tempted to go to Luna's place instead of mine.

But it's the middle of the night and she worked today and...

Despite the marriage license we filed all of a week ago, we're new.

My mouth turns up.

What does the universe consider marriage in Luna's and my case? Date three? Cupcakes in the middle of the night was date one. Meeting—or reconnecting—with my family over pastries was date two. Watching me play, date four. And...then Elvis telling her to kiss her hunka, hunka burning love.

I grin.

So, it's date four.

Tomorrow, I'll see about securing a fifth.

Grinning, I park, grab my shit from the back, and start for the elevators, taking one up to my floor. I step off into the hall, unlock the door to my condo—

And freeze.

"Hey, handsome," I hear.

It's funny, I realize as I look over and see her in the kitchen, not having expected her to use the code I gave her to get inside, certainly not expecting to see her sitting there with two mugs on the counter in front of her, looking adorably sexy in her pajamas. Definitely not expecting her to remember what I'd said all those years ago.

Almost a throwaway, something tossed into the air, half-joking. Back then I didn't realize it actually *does* matter. Even five minutes ago, I would have said this wasn't important.

Until I walked into my condo in the middle of the night, exhaustion creeping in, and...

Found she's done this for me.

"Come in," she says softly, moving my way. She tugs me out of the open doorway, closing and locking it up behind me. Then she's taking my hand, drawing me into the kitchen. "It's silly," she says as she pushes me down gently onto a stool. "This week has been..." Her mouth curves into a half-smile. "More than a little crazy and I...I don't know how to quantify us or what we're doing—"

"We're just us, Luns," I say. "This doesn't need quantifying aside from that."

Her eyes come to mine. "Maybe not." She turns to the opposite counter then rotates back to face me, a mug in each of her hands. "But *I* need it—or at least, I need to feel like I'm not just clinging to your shirttails and making your life complicated."

My heart squeezes. "*Luns.*"

"Because you knew my family then, honey—"

Another pulse through my heart. Because it feels fucking great when she calls me honey.

Her next words don't feel remotely as good, though.

"I talked to my attorney today," she says. "They're getting the ball rolling. Which means that soon enough John and my dad are going to know about the marriage—and that means they're going to know about *you*." She sets the mugs on the counter in front of me and I take advantage of her hands being free to lace my fingers through hers.

"I can handle your dad and brother, sweetheart," I say quietly.

Her expression tells me that she's not so confident about that, but before I can reassure her further, she says, "But I don't want to talk about them tonight."

Me neither.

I don't want to talk at all.

I *want* to—

"I'm struggling," she says and my focus snaps away from my hardening dick, arrowing back to her, worry knotting my insides. "Because it feels like you're doing a lot for me and I'm doing nothing but dropping into your life, creating chaos, and dragging you into my mess."

I open my mouth, but she's still talking.

"You married me, for God's sake!" She pushes out a sharp breath. "And you're giving up your freedom to help me after I broke up with you and we didn't talk for years, and I don't know what kind of person does that—"

I start to speak, but her words keep coming.

"Except that it's *you*," she says, tone softening, eyes gentling, fingers tightening around mine. "It's the Aiden I knew then and the Aiden you are now who I'm only just learning, and I just figured..." Her throat works, fingers tightening further. "While I don't know everything about the man you are today, I do know *my* Aiden, and so—" She waves her free hand to the mugs. "Hot chocolate." A beat. "And someone here to drink it with you."

My heart is suddenly pounding. *"Luns."*

Her voice is gentle. "You said that when your practices ran late and you got home after your siblings were asleep, your mom would wait up for you with hot chocolate."

My pulse speeds.

"She would sit with you and catch up on your day—what went on at school or at the rink—or she'd help you with your homework if you didn't get it all done before then." Luna nudges a mug in my direction. "Or sometimes, she would just sit here and let you talk about practice or off-ice being hard or help you work through whatever your coach yelled at you about on the ice." A soft smile. "And she'd always do it with hot cocoa."

Pulse still speeding, I fill in the rest. "She said hot chocolate took the edge of the day off." My lips twitch. "Now as an adult, I'm half-convinced she drugged it with melatonin so I'd finally chill out and go to sleep."

Luna giggles. "Well, I didn't think about the drugging part —though I do have some melatonin in my purse." A wink that has me chuckling. "And I have my own special touch too." She slips her hand from mine, goes to the fridge, then pulls out a can of whipped cream, squirting an almost obscene amount on both of our hot cocoas. And just when I think she's done, she squirts some more, making us both laugh. "And for the *pièce de résistance...*" She lifts a container of sprinkles, undoes the cap, and liberally douses both of our hot cocoas with the rainbow-colored candies.

"Now drink up," she orders, screwing on the cap and *oh so gently* tracing her finger beneath my healing cut, as though just her touch can mend the injury. And maybe she does have magical healing powers because the nagging ache in my cheek disappears—or maybe it just relocates elsewhere. Somewhere *south.* "Then," she murmurs. "I want you to tell me all about how much of a pain in the ass Smitty was on the way home."

Fuck.

It hits me like a ton of bricks then.

Why I didn't freak out about her showing up, why I didn't even question stepping in and marrying her.

Because we might have spent a decade apart.

But I never stopped loving Luna.

And that doesn't change as we finish our hot cocoa, as I loop my arm around her waist and taste the chocolate treat on her tongue.

As I lift her up and carry her to the bedroom.

Where I love her another way until we're both too exhausted to move.

TWENTY-EIGHT

Luna

"I TRULY AM SO happy for you, my dears!" Kathy exclaims as we descend the steps of the Black family house. "But I need to see the ring again." A wink. "Just to make sure my boy treated you right."

"And because she's like a magpie who likes shiny things," Matt quips, earning himself a swat across the chest.

Grinning, I allow her to draw me to a stop at the end of the walkway, to gather in a little half-circle as I hold up my hand and let Aiden's mom examine my ring for the umpteenth time since we showed up for lunch an hour ago.

The spread of sandwiches and soup, salads and a fruit tart for dessert was delicious.

But Aiden's tired and I got a call from the shelter.

Despite it being my day off, they need me to talk with one of the newer girls who's been staying there—a teenager who is sweet and quiet, but has only opened up to me. Bri is great, but she's been hurt far too often, and if she's reaching out, asking for me, I'm going to talk to her, no matter the hour.

Honestly, I'm a little relieved for the out.

Kathy and Matt have been gracious and understanding, but it's a lot—*Kathy's* a lot. A buzzing tornado of energy.

She genuinely cares.

But I've spent the last few years taking care of Grams after living on my own. I'm not used to this amount of motherly fussing and though I feel a bit like a jerk, I need to up my tolerance of Kathy in small increments, I think.

Grams was nosy, but she had her own life.

Even when she was busy interfering in mine, she was doing her work at Smythe and visiting friends and always working on another project.

Kathy is—

Well, she's different.

Not bad.

But not what I'm used to.

A real mom.

"Beautiful," Kathy murmurs, not looking at my ring, and my heart squeezes.

Because she's looking at me.

Yeah, definitely not what I'm used to.

But I don't stop her from tugging me in for another hug, from her whispering in my ear, "Just like you."

"Thanks," I whisper back.

She hugs me tight then draws back, cupping both of my cheeks. "I'm just glad you're in Aiden's—and our—lives again, no matter how unconventionally that came about." Her mouth curves. "My Aiden has always been one to go his own way, so while you two showing up hitched is a surprise, it's a good one. We're happy to have you in the family, sweetheart."

"You say that now, Mom," Aiden teases. "Just wait until we hit you up to plan the party."

"Party?"

"And why do her eyes light up with glee"—Aiden kisses the top of my head, pulls me back against him—"exactly the same way Smitty's did when I promised he could help if you needed it."

"Oh Smitty is such a dear," Kathy says. "And he loves a party." She tugs her phone out of her pocket. "I'll call him right now, see what ideas he has."

Aiden groans softly, but when I look up, he's smiling. "At least it'll keep them both busy for the foreseeable future," he stage whispers.

My lips quirk.

"Do you need to borrow the truck to move Luna's stuff into your condo?" Matt asks as Kathy starts typing on her phone, presumably texting Smitty for his thoughts on the upcoming party.

"That would be great," Aiden says. "But it'll be us moving my stuff into Luna's place."

My mouth falls open as I turn to him. "What?"

He touches my cheek. "It's Grams's house," he says softly. "Where she taught you to cook and where she and your mom showed you the ropes of Gin Rummy. You have memories there —a lot of really good ones." He shrugs. "Meanwhile, my condo is just a condo."

"But your condo is close to the rink and you said you just bought it—"

"So, I'll sell it or rent it out. Plus, my neighbors are annoying as hell as you know." Another shrug. "Because it has absolutely nothing on her place."

"That's perfect!" Kathy interjects. "I always hated him up in that building. A house is where you make a family, where you settle, not a concrete tower overlooking a busy street. Oh!" She claps her hands together. "We'll have the party celebrating you two there! That way Grams and your mom will feel close to you, Luna."

My heart swells.

See? She's a good person.

Just...a lot.

I grin as she focuses back on her phone, typing furiously and heaven help Smitty for the barrage of messages about to head his way. "If I remember correctly," she says to no one in particular, "the back yard would be perfect for a fall celebration —all of those trees..." She sighs contentedly. "We can put up twinkly lights and it'll be beautiful."

"I—"

The back yard?

Panic starts curling through my insides.

The house is barely together after the repairs—the rooms still full of boxes. Hell, most of the toilets haven't been cleaned since...I don't even know when. I've been slowly—read *slowly*— putting everything to rights, but the back yard is low down on that list, so it's barely been touched.

Oh God.

I shudder at the state of it. It's more weeds than trees at this point.

Grams would kill me if she saw the state of it.

Kathy with her twinkly lights and grand party plans? She'll be disappointed.

And I can't have that.

"Kathy," I hedge. "The house isn't ready—"

Aiden draws me back against his chest, lips coming to my ear. "This is *exactly* the project she needs." A gentle kiss. "Trust me."

"I can't ask her to clean—"

"You're not asking," Kathy says firmly, still typing away on her phone. "I'm volunteering."

"But the back yard is a mess and I only just moved my things into the house. I haven't unpacked or dusted or cleaned toilets. It's a disaster—"

Kathy touches my shoulder. "I have this," she says. "Don't worry. I know you mentioned that work is really busy for you right now—trying to get that new site off the ground and now having to go in on your day off. But just leave it to us!" She takes Matt's hand, practically bouncing with excitement. "We love a project."

Matt's face tells me that's likely not true.

But he just nods, and although it's a bit beleaguered, he draws Kathy close to his side and tells her, "This means I'm getting my new table saw."

Saw?

Saw?

"Oh, good! Smitty told me he's always wanted to learn how to use power tools."

A sinking feeling churning through my stomach, I open my mouth to ask what exactly he's going to need a saw for when a car tears into the driveway, screeching to a halt mere feet from us.

Aiden yanks me behind him, his big body between me and the threat. "What the—?"

I peek out when I hear car doors slam and footsteps echo on the concrete of the driveway.

Then wish I didn't when I see my father and brother stalking toward us.

The latter jabs a finger in my direction.

"You conniving little bitch!"

TWENTY-NINE

Aiden

RIGHT.

Well, I haven't seen John Maybelle in more than ten years.

And even putting aside him calling his sister a bitch, I could take one look at the fucker and know that he's an asshole.

Screwed up expression.

Ugly ass polo and fucking chinos, for God's sake.

Giant, ostentatious watch.

Hair that has more product in it than Gray's does on picture day—and my captain is one of the few guys on the roster who actually takes the time to style his hair for team photos.

Probably because those dumb things are shown on TV over and over again throughout the season.

But Gray taking the time once in a while to do his hair doesn't mean he wears loafers.

John sure as shit does—and his loafers have fucking tassels on them.

They swing slightly as the dumbass marches my way.

Christ, what an idiot.

"Mom?" I say.

"Um," she replies, quietly for a change, "is that who I think that is?"

There's another slam and I tear my gaze from the douche canoe who is Luna's brother to see that this situation is about to get worse.

Because Luna's dad is here.

In a three-piece suit, as much crap in his hair as his son, his dress shoes clicking on the pavement as he starts toward us.

"Mom," I say again, a little sharper this time, knowing that I need to get her to focus.

I see her startle slightly out of the corner of my eye, then feel Luna do the same when I say, "Get Luna inside, yeah? Dad and I will handle this."

Luna snags my hand, squeezes slightly. "Aiden, I—"

"You bitch!" John snaps again.

I tug my hand free, plunk it in the middle of the asshole's chest, stopping him in his tracks—or maybe sending him back a few paces...

Right.

Okay more than a *few*.

But I don't have time to worry about some asshole nearly eating shit in my parents' driveway.

I need to move quickly.

My eyes lock with my mom's, and I tilt my head toward the house.

Thankfully, she snaps out of her surprise, takes Luna's arm, and draws her inside.

I hear the front door close, lock, and exhale, stuffing down my temper and bracing myself to deal with the asshole contingent of the Blacks.

Luna's dad, Frank, if I remember correctly, brushes by his son, who's still straightening after fighting to regain his balance. And Frank does that brushing without so much as asking his son if he's okay.

Great parenting.

But it's not like I expect anything different.

Assholes raise assholes.

The only reason that Luna escaped the same fate was that Frank didn't give two shits about his daughter so left her to Grams to raise after his wife died.

Thank God.

I got Luns, *my* Luns.

And the asshole contingent stayed far away...

Until now.

"I'm guessing that Luna's lawyers reached out to you," I say dryly, feeling my dad twitch beside me.

I'll have to explain later.

For now, I've got bigger problems.

John's face scrunches up again and he turns bright fucking red—and fuck if the asshole doesn't look like an adult-sized toddler.

But it's Frank who speaks, tilting his head, gray irises that are the same color as Luna's but don't have a lick of the warmth as hers locking onto me, studying me like the beady-eyed snake he is.

"Aiden Black," he says cooly.

I extend my hand for him to shake—the man is my father-in-law after all—but he merely shifts his stare to it, and after a moment, I let it fall to my side.

So, we're not going to pretend to be nice.

Kinda figured that after his son called my woman a bitch, but it's always better to try, right?

Or maybe not, I think when Frank shoves a sheaf of papers in my direction.

"What's this?" I say, barely catching them against my chest.

"Divorce papers," he snaps. "I'll expect them to be signed and returned to my office tomorrow."

My dad grunts from beside me, but I can't spare him a glance.

Because I'm too busy trying not to throttle the fuckers in front of me.

"Yeah, no," I say, shoving them the papers back at him, taking more than a little bit of satisfaction when he scrambles to not drop them. "That's not going to happen."

Frank's fat fingers close around the papers, crinkling the load of them as he shoves them at John, who's finally recovered enough to join the grownups in conversation.

Unfortunately, his reflexes aren't as quick as mine or even his dad's.

Because the entire stack of them goes flying, the wind catching them, sending them off in all directions.

Works for me.

"Right," I mutter, catching my dad's eyes and hitching my head in the direction of the house. "That seems like as good a place as any to end this conversation."

My dad nods and I know he and my mom are going to demand an explanation for this scene—and likely the whole getting married so Luna can save the world thing that, while noble, isn't going to go over all that well.

My mom's a romantic.

My dad's pragmatic.

Taking on the Maybelles, no matter how noble, or how much I like—*love*—Luna isn't a shitstorm they're going to want me to endure.

Good thing I'm an adult.

Because I'm not letting Luna go, not again, not when I just got her back.

I shouldn't have let her slip away in the first place.

But that's a regret for another day.

My dad turns for the house, hitching his head for me to follow. But when I do, I'm stopped by a big, meaty hand on my shoulder.

And I don't think.

I just react.

Poorly.

Whipping around, I grab John's wrist and twist, shoving him back against the porch pillar. "Don't touch me, you prick." I step closer, my face an inch away from his. "And stay the fuck away from Luna or—"

"Or what?" I hear Frank Maybelle say.

I twist my neck, see that he's watching me closely, a calculating expression on his face.

"Or you'll make threats?" he drawls. "Whatever will the Grizzlies think of that?" He taps a finger to his chin. "What will they think of one of their players harming an innocent man?"

Innocent.

Ha.

That's a fucking joke.

My hand tightens.

John cries out in pain.

I should keep going, show his Frank what it feels like too...

"Aiden," my dad says quietly.

And I hear the warning in his tone, know that he's right.

Of course he's right.

I can't pummel John and/or Frank Maybelle into a pulp, no matter how much they may deserve it.

Damn.

Slowly, I peel my fingers my fingers from John's wrist, taking no little amount of pleasure in the fact that he winces and clutches his arm to his chest. "You'll regret this," he snaps, glaring at me.

"Maybe," I tell him. "But at least—at the end of the day—I know I'm not the one throwing away something as precious as Luna."

THIRTY

Luna

"JUST BREATHE, HONEY," Kathy says, slowly smoothing her hand up and down my back.

"I should go out and talk to them." The words sound a lot surer than I feel, mostly because I'm shaking, my stomach in knots.

I'm used to the way they talk to me, used to the vitriol and rage.

What if they tell Aiden something truly awful?

What if he *believes* them?

What if my part of the curse isn't to die young like Becky, my sister, like my mom, but to be like Grams—alone and left behind, living without the man I love for the majority of my adult years.

Wishing things had gone differently.

That circumstances could have been altered.

And knowing there was nothing I could do to change it.

I close my eyes, hate that a tear slips free, slides down my cheek.

"It'll be okay," Kathy murmurs and my lids peel back when she wipes gently beneath one set of lashes and then the other. "I promise."

It's sweet of her to say that, beyond kind.

But I can't stop the sinking feeling in my belly that this has all gone too easy before now—Aiden accepting my reappearance, us getting married, the sex, him knowing instinctively that I wouldn't want to give up Grams's place—and I'm worried this is going to blow up in my face, no matter how much I need, and *want,* it to work out.

Doing something better.

Having Aiden in my life.

Having...something more.

Something that means *everything*.

And an everything that slides just out of reach.

"How do you know it'll be okay?" I whisper, heart squeezing painfully.

"Because you know as well as I do," she says, "that when Aiden says he'll take care of it, he'll *take care* of it."

I *do* know that.

He's the one person in my life who has never *ever* failed me.

If anyone can handle my brother and father, he can.

The only question is—why should he have to?

Stifling a groan, I blink the tears away and whisper, "Yes, he will."

"Exactly, honey." She cups my cheek. "I see you're getting it now."

"It's just...it's not that simple," I whisper.

A gentle smile. "I can promise you that the Black men are simple when it comes to the women they love."

My heart squeezes again and then the words just...slip out. "But it's not like you think, Kathy."

A long pause before she asks, "What do you mean, sweetheart?"

Shit.

Yet, I can't stop myself from admitting, "We didn't just get married because we're in love and reconnected after all these years."

Her mouth curves and it's so much like Aiden's smile that my lungs hitch, but the movement, my words, don't have her releasing me. Instead, she holds me a little tighter, brushes back the hair from my face. "I figured as much."

My mouth drops open. "You did?"

She nods. "Like I said, Aiden goes his own way. But eloping is out there, even for him." A beat. "Especially in the middle of the season."

I wince. "Right," I whisper.

Because he would have timed it better.

Of course he would have.

"So," I whisper, "you shouldn't spend money or time on the party, on Grams's back yard. Aiden's doing me a favor—*did* me a favor by marrying me—but we don't need a party and you definitely shouldn't put yourself out to celebrate our marriage."

She's quiet again for a long moment. Then, "He did you a favor?"

I hesitate, shame eating at my insides, but I know I owe her an explanation, owe her the truth. "When Grams died..." I put my pride aside and tell her all about Grams's will, about the shares, about wanting to do something better with all that Smythe is, watching her face carefully as I speak, worry knotting my insides as I search for any sign of disappointment, of disgust, of despair.

Because her son deserves more.

"It's really wonderful he's doing this for me," I whisper. "But I should have stopped things from going this far, should have known that the curse would have struck—" My throat stoppers up, words caught so tightly they can't keep escaping.

"Um, honey," she murmurs after several seconds. "I don't want to interject when you're being so open, but you've given me a lot of information here—information that all makes sense...all of it except whatever this is about a curse."

Dammit.

I'm an idiot.

And one look at her face tells me that she's not going to let this go.

And maybe...I just need to finally tell someone.

Exhaling, I stare into green eyes that are similar to Aiden's, except with more gold flecks. "You're going to think I'm ridiculous," I hedge.

"There's nothing ridiculous about any of this." She takes my hand. "Now, sweetheart, tell me about the curse."

My gaze slides to the side, still delaying, but the part of me that needs to tell someone has grown, taking over, and I release another breath, the truth slipping free. "I remember hearing about it for the first time when my mom was telling her best friend that Maybelle women are cursed with one of three fates —to choose their partners poorly, to die young, or to be left behind pining for the men they love but who don't love them back."

"Honey—"

"Or *worse* to be cursed to live all three." I shake my head. "I know it sounds stupid, and I remember being old enough, having read enough books, having seen enough Disney movies to think that happy endings were guaranteed, that curses didn't really exist—or at the very least, that curses were meant to be broken by heroes with hearts of gold and really great hair and smiles that never fail to make the fair maidens melt." Her hand tightens around mine, as though she instinctively knows that something bad is going to happen.

And she's right.

"Then my mom died in the car accident and my sister spent all those months in the hospital before she eventually passed away too, and I started to believe in the curse. Two Maybelles, two victims of the curse." I press my lips together. "And eventually I realized Grams was a victim too—she chose poorly, picking my grandfather, who only spent long enough with her to make my dad before going right back to his mistress. She waited for almost forty years wishing for him to come home, pining away and living a life that wasn't fully for herself. And that pattern has continued back for generations—my aunt was left at the altar, my great grandmother died in childbirth, taking her youngest daughter with her, my cousin's husband took her for every bit of her worth, leaving her homeless until Grams stepped in, and..." I sigh. "The list goes on and on and *on*. Every woman in my family has the same story—we're cursed when it comes to love."

"But not you."

I rub at my forehead. "Because I had absolutely no intention of putting myself in the curse's crosshairs." I glance at my lap, admit, "It's why I pushed Aiden away when we were teenagers. Why I couldn't so much step foot in the rink after he left to play juniors—too many memories, too much temptation to reach out again, too high of a risk if I did."

Her fingers wrap around mine. "I don't blame you for keeping your distance, sweetheart."

My eyes fly to hers, shock rippling through me. "You don't?"

"With that family track record," she says dryly, "it's no wonder that you were a little gun shy." She straightens, shakes her head. "I can almost see why your Grams felt like she needed to give you a push. Now is it the way I would have gone about it? No—" Her lips twitch. "Okay, fine. I actually think it's pretty brilliant. I definitely would have done something like that, especially if it meant that the granddaughter I loved would finally step off the sidelines of her life and start living."

"I—"

But I can't finish the sentence.

Because I think I finally might understand a bit about why Grams did what she did.

Trust the process, break the curse, and know I love you so, so much.

Maybe she truly didn't believe in the Maybelle Curse.

Maybe she gave me this push so I wouldn't end up alone.

Maybe...

The future I've dreamed of—the fantasy, the dashing hero, the happy ending—can actually be mine.

"Thank you," I whisper, tucking those realizations close, the wound in my heart slightly smaller for the first time ever.

"For what?"

"For making it make sense."

Expression gentling, she bumps her shoulder against mine. "Thank you for sharing this with me." Another squeeze of her fingers. "For sharing *all* of it."

"I have to admit"—the words just flow out of me, probably imprudently but also, I don't have any hope of stopping their flow, not now that I've let this all come out—"I worried I might not know how to handle you and Carrie."

Kathy laughs. "Why's that?"

"Because you guys are so..." I was going to say *much*, but that's rude, yet the delay of me searching for a word that *isn't* rude (and coming up blank) has her laughing. "I'm used to Grams," I blather, "but she wasn't like you guys—your family is so close, and you all know so much about each other. And you're so comfortable in yourselves. I don't think Grams or I have ever had that."

If Grams had, she wouldn't have spent years pining away for a man who hurt her over and over again.

And I wouldn't have spent far too long letting my father and brother walk all over me, wouldn't have pushed Aiden away because I was scared we wouldn't work out.

Only...he's not away now, is he?

My heart flutters, but before I can truly sit in that thought, she's speaking again, "You know the one rejoinder I've heard my whole life?"

I shake my head.

"That I'm always too loud, too brash, too *much*." She shrugs. "Quiet down. Make yourself smaller. Fit in. Over and over again—" A sigh. "But eventually, as I got older, the words everyone kept telling me stopped meaning so much. I finally realized that I am who I am and..." Another shrug. "I'm not going to apologize for that any longer."

Guilt wraps itself tightly around my heart. "I'm sorry."

"For stating the truth?" She tucks a strand of my hair behind my ear. "Don't be. It's reminded me that while I am who I am, that *is* a lot." A tap to the tip of my nose. "So, it's important to go slowly and say"—her mouth curves—"*not* force fed my son's new wife pastries until she's ready to burst."

I giggle. "For the record, they're delicious so I wasn't exactly complaining."

"Because you were too full to get the words out?"

I giggle again. "Maybe."

She touches my cheek, eyes going serious. "Want something else that's *for the record?*"

"Sure," I murmur.

"Life's not full of fairytales, sweetheart."

My heart pulses but she goes on before I can speak.

"But if there is ever a prince and princess who can break an evil curse, it's you and Aiden."

THIRTY-ONE

Aiden

"YEAH, YEAH, YEAH!" I call, streaking toward the net.

Gray spots me, dekes around one of the Eagles and flicks the pass my way.

It flies through the air, dropping just in time to land on my stick as I cut to the net.

Two defenseman stand between me and the goal, but that's okay, Gray's following his pass and Ryan's on his heels.

We have numbers.

We have a little bit of time.

We have space.

I stay wide, trying to draw one of the defenseman to me, but my opponent is on to my tactics, staying between me and his net, leaving me with a tough angle to connect a pass back over to my teammates.

It's the right play since I generally prefer to make the pass over the shot—the high I get from creating a great play much higher than picking a corner or slipping a puck through the goalie's five-hole.

But I *can* score.

And if the opportunity presents itself then I'm not going to allow it to pass me by.

I cut in around him before I run out of room, taking a sharp right to the net, dragging the puck with me in a move I've only fucked around with during practice—

Around the tip of the defenseman's stick, sliding it between his feet.

Then off the heel of one of my skates…

And kicking it up onto the tip of *my* stick.

Then it's just me and the goalie and I'm only five feet away, four, *three*—

I deke to the right with my shoulders and, at the same time, I release the top hand on my stick.

So, I'm in close, holding onto my twig with my weaker hand, the other D is closing in rapidly, and the puck almost out of reach.

That's okay though.

I keep faking right, keep drawing the goalie that direction.

Not much—he's too good, too smart, too fast.

But I get him to bite an inch.

And that's enough.

I grunt as I stretch that final centimeter, managing to use the very tip of my stick to push the puck forward, to slide it…

Into that open inch.

I have exactly one heartbeat to watch the puck slide over the goal line before I'm shoved hard from behind—

And then I'm eating ice.

But I don't give a fuck because the goal horn is blasting and the Grizzlies' celebratory song is blaring through the arena's speakers and Smitty is hauling me up from the ice and hugging me tight. "Fuck yeah, man!" he says, squeezing all the air from my lungs. "That was *sick!*"

He pounds me on the back, almost as hard as I was just crosschecked, pushing any of the air I just managed to suck in right back out of my lungs.

"Thanks," I croak as we start skating to the bench, slipping out of reach and taking a second to breathe.

Then I'm skating along the boards, fist-bumping my teammates, knowing that I'm grinning wide.

I can't believe that shit worked.

But I'll take it.

"Nice, man," Ryan says as we pause by the open door and he stops to let me go ahead of him. "Really fucking nice."

I nod my thanks, sit my tired ass on the bench and slide down to make room for the rest of my linemates.

Once we're settled, Gray—as effusive as ever—lifts his hand for me to fist bump. "Killer," he says. Then half his mouth quirks up. "Now let's get one more."

A word of praise.

Then right back to work.

If that doesn't describe my captain then I don't know what does.

I nod, fist bump him back, and then I focus on the game...

And by the end of the third, I don't manage to score another goal, but I do manage to tally assists on two more of them.

We beat the Eagles for the first time this season.

I'm pulled aside to do press—answering questions about my goal, about my assists on the Gray's and Ryan's subsequent goals.

My replies are nothing special—just the usual statements about there being many more games this season and that we need to continue to work hard and grind out our wins—but the questions aren't all that special either.

Still, it *is* pretty cool to see the replay on my goal.

Because that shit *was* sick.

"Thanks, guys," I tell our post-game commentators before the camera feed cuts away and I take off my headphones, handing them back to the production staff, extending my thanks to them as well before I start down the hall.

Shower. Cool down routine.

Then back to my condo.

Because tomorrow we're packing my shit up.

And the day after, we're bringing it over to Grams's house—or well, Luna's and my house now. The team has two days off, one more home game, and then another short road trip.

I want to be moved in before I head out for that trip, want to make sure Luns isn't exposed to her brother and father without me being there—the first is doable, the second...well, I'm still working on that portion of the plan.

Kind of hard to protect her when I'm on the road.

Shaking my head, I turn for the locker room, but before I can push through the door, a traffic jam of people has me halting, trying to find the source of the backup.

Ah.

A pair of cameras point at an older man in a suit—and it only takes me a couple of seconds for me to recognize him as Jean-Michel Dubois, the owner of the Eagles, Oak Ridge Vineyards, and Titan Capital—a local firm that has invested in many Bay Area companies...including several charities.

I make a mental not to tell Luna that—if I remember correctly, he funds several animal rescue foundations that focus on saving and rehoming dogs and cats—but I've also heard that he has a soft spot for the women in his life, including his daughter, Chrissy, and his woman, Tiff.

Maybe Luna could approach him for a donation to help fund the second location for the shelter.

He scowls at me as I slip by, intent on the locker room's door.

Or *maybe* she should wait a few days, like when the win and my goal aren't being shown on the highlight reels.

Smothering my smile—because, yeah, I like to make a play, a pass, rack up those assists, but that goal—especially knowing that Luns was watching at home—feels good as hell.

"Black?" I hear as I start to push into the Grizzlies' locker room.

I pause, glance back over my shoulder.

Jean-Michel's gaze hits mine...and his lips curve into the barest hint of a smile. "Nice goal."

"Thanks," I say, turning away again, losing my fight on my smile.

Then freeze again.

Because I hear, "But you only get one."

Chuckling, I shake my head and then—probably imprudently—I toss back, "We'll see."

THIRTY-TWO

Luna

I'M RUNNING LATE, heading out of my office, an itchy feeling between my shoulder blades.

Because I've haven't heard a peep from my father and my brother.

And it's been nearly two weeks since they appeared at Kathy and Matt's place, shouting and angry...and then leaving after Aiden confronted them.

My family doesn't just leave—absolutely not.

They dig their heels in, stay in place, unmovable by even the most intense of mother nature's forces.

And then they dig in a little further.

But not that day.

They just...left.

And haven't come back—leaving me with the sinking feeling that they're going to show up sooner rather than later, and most likely, at the most inopportune time.

Sighing, I rub my temple, hoping to ease the ache there, knowing that it's no use to try to make sense of their actions. I'm not going to be able to figure them out, and anyway, I know their motives, know their end goals, know they won't give up until they get what they want—

So, yeah. They'll be around again.

Mostly likely at the worst possible moment.

Sighing again, I grab my purse from the bottom drawer of my desk then turn and start down the hall.

Only to be stopped by Marissa, one of the shelter's volunteers.

"Do you have a minute?" she asks after waving me to a stop.

I nod. "Of course. What's up?"

"It's Bri."

Damn. After what happened at Kathy's and Matt's, I didn't have a chance to catch up with her—by the time I got here, she was gone and she hasn't been in since. "Right," I say. "How can I help?"

"She finally came back in today, and she doesn't look good," Marissa murmurs. "She's covered in bruises and if she had a full meal in the last two weeks, I'd be shocked."

Less damn and more *shit*. "Is she talking to anyone?"

A shake of her head. "No," Marissa says on a sigh. "She just clams up every time someone asks—just gets her food, gets her shower and a few nights of good sleep, and then, she's gone again."

I exhale. "Right," I whisper. "I'll try to talk to her."

"She can have a permanent bed here if she wants. And there's an opening at the bakery—it's just for sales during the morning shift, but if she has an interest in something in particular, we can work toward making that happen," Marissa tells me, and God, this is why I love this place. We do our best to change things, to make good happen.

"Right," I say. "I'll see if she's open to any of that."

"Thanks, Luna."

I nod and exchange my goodbyes then head through the double doors that lead to the youth center.

Bri's in her usual corner, curled in on herself as she reads a book.

And the sight of the bruise on her cheekbone makes me want to commit murder—here I am worried about rich people problems of inheritance and company control, and she's living a nightmare.

I push down the guilt, the fury, and pause near an open chair next to her. "Cool if I sit here?"

She jumps, eyes flicking up from the book for only a second before they go right back to the page—and Christ, the bruise is bad. So bad it starts my rage boiling again.

"Whatever," she says after a long moment.

Not exactly a ringing endorsement, but I take the empty chair, pick up the book I started the last time Bri and I sat here, exactly like this, words few and far between—but still more with me than anyone else—and begin reading.

The book is a good one, a young adult novel featuring a broody hero, a sassy heroine, and there's plenty of magic, yearning and angst, and kickass fight scenes.

So even though it takes a full chapter for Bri to break, I'm not impatient.

"You don't have to do this, you know?" she mutters.

I keep my place on the page with a fingertip and glance over at Bri. "Clue me in on what exactly it is that I'm doing?"

"Trying to make sure I'm okay " She lifts one bony shoulder then drops it. "I'm fine."

"Aside from the fact that you have a bruise the size of a grapefruit on your cheek?"

Her shoulders hitch up and she scowls. "It's nothing."

"It's *something*," I tell her. "But, as always, you don't have to share anything you don't want to." Those shoulders relax slightly and she exhales in relief. "There's a bed here that can be yours permanently, and a job in the bakery if you want it."

Something flickers through her eyes and I think, for a second, that I'm actually getting through to her.

Then she shrugs, says, "I'm fine."

I stifle a sigh, but know that little flicker in her eyes is a chip in the thick shield around her, that I'm slowly getting through, that eventually we'll get somewhere.

Eventually.

I have to believe it will be eventually and not never.

Otherwise...*no*. I can't think about what might happen to this girl if it's *never*.

Still, for today, I know that flicker is likely all I'm going to get. She's a tough cookie and I've barely scratched the surface of her and—

"You got married?"

I jerk, nearly drop my book.

Then look up at her. She's staring at my ring. "Yes," I say softly. "A few weeks back."

"I didn't know you had a boyfriend."

That's because I didn't.

"His name is Aiden," I tell her instead of that. "He plays for the Grizzlies."

Nothing. Her face is a blank mask.

"The NHL team."

A long pause. "I know."

Right. Okay then. "Do you want to see a picture of him?"

I don't mind staring at that gorgeous face of him and maybe sharing this piece of me will get her to share in return.

"No."

The word is spoken tersely enough that I immediately change tactics.

No boy talk. Got it.

"Okay," I say easily. "How's school going?"

"Same as always. Teachers are dicks sometimes. Kids are assholes." She scowls. "But I like my history class."

My lips quirk. "What's different about history compared to the others?"

Suspicion in her eyes, but when I don't press her further, she gives me a little something. "He doesn't just make us memorize shit. He tells stories, and they're interesting sometimes."

Interesting...sometimes.

My lips twitch again.

"What type of history is it?" I ask. "U.S. History? Or World History? Or something else I can't think of because my history teachers were supremely boring and most of the time just made us memorize dates of battles and what general was fighting for what side."

"That sounds lame."

"It was."

I feel like cheering when her mouth turns up, then again when she gives me a glimpse of her wicked sense of humor. "When was that again?" she teases. "The Stone Age?"

I nudge her foot with mine. "Rude." A beat. "It was clearly the Bronze Age."

She laughs.

Fuck, yeah.

Then answers, which is even better. "It's World History. I like Mr. Crenshaw's stories about Ancient Egypt."

I nod sagely. "Objectively the best part of World History."

"Exactly."

Our gazes lock and I hold my breath—the flicker in her eyes

has grown, emotions I can't read swirling in the rich brown depths. Maybe she'll take the permanent bed? The job?

But she doesn't speak.

Just glances back down to her book.

And, deflated, I follow a heartbeat later.

We read in silence for long moments, the draw of the teenage angst slightly tempered.

This girl deserves more, deserves—

"What was your favorite subject in school?"

My fingers tighten on my book at the quiet question, hope and frustration, rage and softness all tangled together.

I want to push her to open up.

I want to demand she take action to make herself safe.

I know that will get me nowhere.

So, I go back to our usual—humor.

"Back in the Stone Age?"

"I thought it was the Bronze Age?" She giggles.

"PE," I say after I've soaked up the joyous sound of her laughter. "Followed closely by science."

"Probably why you married the hockey player," she mutters, flipping to the next page in her book.

"No," I tell her baldly, knowing that no matter how complicated the circumstance of my marriage are, she needs to hear this, she needs to understand that her reality isn't the only future that exists. And maybe…I need to remind myself of it too. "I married Aiden because I've been in love with him since I was thirteen and he's the one person in my life who's never let me down."

She closes her book and sets it to the side. "Really?"

"Really." My heart is pounding. It's the truth, but it's a big one, a scary one. Still, I nod at her, closing my book too. "We lost touch for a bit when he went off to play professionally, but now that we've both been in the same city, we reunited. And…

it's the same—he always was my best friend, the one person who saw me as me. He's all of that and more now too."

"What about your Grams?" she asks, her eyes going a bit suspicious. "I thought you two were close."

"We were. So close that I still miss her every day." My voice cracks and I clear my throat. "But the truth is that while Grams loved me and I *really* loved her, neither of us were perfect and sometimes"—like, say, with the whole get married to get her shares thing—"I think that her past influenced *my* future far too much."

Bri is quiet for a moment.

Then says with far too much certainty, "I can see how that could happen."

"Yeah," I tell her softly. "I know you do."

We're quiet for a long moment.

Those flickers in her eyes growing, filling the brown depths, softening them.

So, I take a chance to ask, "Do you want me to tell Marissa you'll think about the bed and the job?"

And it feels like another victory when she nods slightly, mutters, "Yeah."

So...I take another chance.

I write the address to Gram's place on my business card. "We're having a party next Saturday afternoon. I'd love for you to come and meet Aiden."

She nibbles at her bottom lip, but takes the rectangle of paper. "I don't know," she whispers, but at least she tucks the card into her pocket and doesn't yeet it straight into the trash or something.

"No pressure." I say, sensing she's had enough for today and starting to gather up my stuff. "But there will be cake."

Her eyes light up.

Because it's cake.

It's delicious.

And maybe because I haven't forgotten that it's her favorite food.

I wave goodbye, head out to my car, and I do it with my heart a little lighter.

Because I'm going home to someone who knows mine too.

THIRTY-THREE

Aiden

WELL, the second game of our home-and-home matchup against the Eagles didn't go quite as well as night one.

The Eagles take this one, but we'll play each other a total of eight times this season, so it's not over yet.

We'll get them next time.

Hopefully.

Because I know it'll be a struggle to go more than five hundred with them. They're a tough team, tenacious and focused and every game with them is a battle.

Doesn't mean I'm going to give up, though.

Never give up, never surrender.

My mouth hitches up at the obscure movie line—one I wonder if Luns will remember, since we watched the film together as teenagers—and I toss my bag over my shoulder, head out of the locker room.

Time to go home to my woman—something that's a hell of a

lot more convenient when I merely have to drive home instead of getting on a bus and then a plane and then make the drive.

My phone buzzes the moment I hit the hall.

I pull it out, smile widening when I see it's my tiny tornado.

> LUNA: Tough loss tonight, big guy. But nice playing.

> AIDEN: Did I do enough to earn hot cocoa?

> LUNA: ...

> LUNA: Sure. But you might have some work to do before I bust out the whipped cream.

I laugh, start to pocket my phone, but it buzzes again.

> LUNA: And unfortunately, I have to meet with the legal team tomorrow. My dad and brother are throwing up more roadblocks.

My amusement poofs away like so much smoke.

Damn.

> AIDEN: I'm sorry, sweetheart. That sucks, and even though we expected it, that doesn't make things easier.

> LUNA: Yeah.

> AIDEN: I'll be home soon, but I can stop by The Dairy, bring you a pint of that cinnamon swirl ice cream you like?

> LUNA: I don't think I'm in the mood for ice cream. But I could use one of your hugs.

AIDEN: Consider it done.

I shove my phone away, start down the hall, but when I turn into the corridor that leads to the players' parking lot I'm waylaid by a billionaire.

Or in actuality, I nearly plow one down.

"Sorry," I say to Jean-Michel Dubois as he snags my shoulder and steadies me.

"All good, Aiden." His expression fills with humor. "Or should I say, A-man?"

I roll my eyes. "Yeah, I definitely got the short end of the stick on the nickname front. But there's no helping it. Hockey locker rooms do as hockey locker rooms do."

He grins, claps me on the arm. "That's true enough." He starts to step by me then pauses. "Nice game tonight—though I am glad we shut you down."

"There's always next time."

A quirk of his mouth. "Also, true enough." He nods, starts to walks off.

I do the same.

Then remember who I've been talking to—*who* I've been talking to. Jean-Michel Dubois—billionaire with a soft spot for women, who does charity work, and who has a really good, a *really fucking* good legal team.

"Hey, uh, Jean-Michel?" I ask as I spin back around.

He's been pulled into another conversation, but my question has him stopping, looking up. "Yeah, Aiden?"

"I'm sorry to interrupt, I just...do you think I could set up a time to talk with you"—my eyes slant to the man he was speaking to and I try to find the right words because I don't want Luna's business casually tossed through the arena's hallways—"it's not about hockey, but it's...uh...complicated."

Blue eyes lock on mine, studying me like he can see the depths of my soul.

And it doesn't take long before I'm one second away from spilling my guts about everything from the time I stole a candy bar at the grocery store to the unholy dreams I had about Luna during my teenage years to the fact that one of his own players on the Eagles, Hudson, showed me the filthy move that earned me that killer goal in the last game.

Before any of that slips out, he glances over at the man he'd been speaking to. "I'll catch up with you in a few minutes, yeah?"

The man just nods then disappears without another look.

"Does this require privacy?" Jean-Michel says quietly.

I consider that, but he spots the answer—affirmative—before I verbalize it, inclining his head and turning away, leaving me no choice but to follow him around the corner and through a series of hallways before stopping outside a closed door.

He turns the handle, pushes it open, and holds it so I can follow him inside.

Then he leans back against the desk inside the office. "All right, kid. My spidey senses are telling me this is both really good and really bad, and...is also likely to create a fuck-ton more work for me."

I wince.

Because that pretty much sums it up.

But then because I'm critically aware of how busy this man is—and how much more he makes than me per hour, per minute, per *second*, how every moment I'm standing here like a dumbass is a waste of all of those resources.

So, I pull my head together.

And I start talking.

And pretty soon, I tell him everything.

And pretty soon...I know I made the right decision.

Because I've found an ally.

And he happens to be one of the biggest and most powerful men in the world.

Take that, Smythe.

THIRTY-FOUR

Luna

"WHAT DO YOU THINK ABOUT THIS?" Kathy asks, holding up the flower arrangement for the umpteenth time for me to approve.

I open my mouth, intending on saying the same thing as the last ten times she's asked—that it's lovely—but then her lips twitch.

"I'm kidding," she says, setting the vase filled with cheerful autumn flowers on the counter then bumping her shoulder against mine. "And I'll stop torturing you."

Guilt winds through my middle. "You're not—"

A mock frown. "Don't even try it, kiddo."

"I'm not," I tell her, snagging her hand after she spends several moments centering the vase in the island, turning it this way and that, choosing the perfect position to best show off the blooms. "Kathy," I say, squeezing her fingers, waiting until she looks at me then holding her gaze, wanting to be certain she knows I'm serious. "I've spent the last months overwhelmed by repairs and funeral arrangements, packing up Gram's things into boxes and cleaning up construction dust," I murmur. "Because before that, the only thing I could focus on was making sure she was getting better—and then when we both realized that wasn't going happen, all my time was filled with making sure she was comfortable and stowing away enough positive memories that I'd have them for the rest of my life."

"Honey," she whispers, eyes glimmering with tears

"When I moved back to Rockfield, I thought it would be temporary, that she would be living in this house again, buzzing around the kitchen, meddling in my life, being a shield between my brother and dad and me." I sigh. "That didn't happen, obviously. We moved her into my dad's place to complete the repairs her and *I* became the barrier between them and her. And I couldn't think about anything *except* her and work, so that's part of why—" I nod toward the rest of the house. "It was in such shambles."

Kathy snags my hang. "It wasn't that bad—"

"Gram would have been so embarrassed," I murmur. "The dust and boxes, the state of her kitchen and yard, the fact that I was sleeping where I was sleeping. But making this place mine instead of hers...it was accepting that she wasn't here anymore, that everything was different."

Kathy sucks in a breath, apology in her eyes.

"I'm not saying this for any other reason than to let you know that your help over the last couple of weeks has really meant a lot." I squeeze her fingers again. "You've helped me bring back Grams, but also..." I sweep my hand around the kitchen, repainted and sparkling clean, the towels hanging from the oven and over the end of the sink a cheerful bright blue. They match the rugs and new towels in the bathrooms, complement the area rugs and runners in the hall and the living room, the blankets in the master bedroom.

All of which I came home to.

All of which is too much and I argued with Kathy about spending so much money on me.

All of which...I gave in to.

Because I don't have enough money in my account to pay her back—though my lawyers say that, for better or worse, I should have access to my share of the family trust fund soon enough. I'll figure out how to deal with that—with the guilt of dirty money, with protecting myself while doing something good with it—another day.

And anyway, money or not, Kathy refused to accept absolutely anything aside from a hug anyway.

I'll find another way to repay her.

"But you also made this house mine and Aiden's," I finish. "And I can't thank you enough for that. Especially considering the circumstances of our marriage—"

Her face is gentle, but her tone isn't. "Just because you two haven't begun in a traditional way..."

I snort because that's the understatement of the year and she nudges me in the side with her finger.

"Behave," she orders. "But just because it's not traditional doesn't mean that I'm going to give you up, sweetie. In case you missed it, I like you, peanut, and you might have slipped from our grasp once, but us Blacks don't plan on letting that happen a second time."

Butterflies fluttering through my belly. "Is that coming from you or Aiden?"

She grins. "Both of us." A beat. "Separately." Her grin widens. "And together."

That should probably be creepy.

A lot.

But it's also sweet.

And it's Kathy.

"I missed you," I murmur, drawing her into a hug. "But I'm also glad we get to know each other now." My voice is watery and my eyes start to sting.

"Me too," she says, and I don't miss that she's choked up either. "And sweetie, we'll talk about you pushing us away— now *and* then—but on another day. One we're not punctuating with cake."

Fear slides through my insides—talking about that is a terrifying notion.

She touches my cheek. "Be brave, kiddo," she whispers. "Be yourself. And don't be afraid to grab on to your happiness."

I exhale, those tears rising, my lungs threatening to hitch on a sob. "Kathy—"

"You're going to change the world." A tug of my ponytail. "You can handle a conversation."

But can I?

"You can," she answers the unspoken question. "You *can.*"

Then she hugs me tight, and in her arms, I think that maybe she's right, maybe I can, maybe I *am* strong enough.

Maybe it's less than me actually *being* strong enough and more having people on my side who believe I am.

"Thanks, Kathy."

"Anytime, my beautiful girl."

I sniff.

She sniffs.

Luckily, before we can devolve into tears and leave the rest of the flowers we need to arrange for the party celebrating Aiden and me to wilt, there's a knock at the door.

"I'll get it," Kathy says, dashing a finger beneath each eye. "And then we'll finish the party prep."

"Great," I say dryly, earning a light punch on my shoulder before she disappears out of the kitchen. I start opening packets of paper plates and napkins, putting plastic utensils into a little organizer that Kathy brought over.

It's paper and not porcelain, plastic and not stainless steel, maybe not something that my brother or father would think is appropriate, but I love it.

The colors, the care, the fact that we're having food catered in from Aiden's favorite barbecue restaurant, that our cake is flavored with hot cocoa and topped with marshmallow cream frosting.

It's us—the *new* us, the beginning of Aiden and me.

No secrets. No shame. No hiding.

No—

"Luna dear, someone is here to see you."

I still, worry creeping along my spine—thinking that *someone* could be my dad, my brother, here to create chaos—but that worry only lasts a moment. Mostly because I don't hear any yelling and because Kathy didn't slam the door, leaving them to rot on the porch, so it *can't* be my dad or brother.

When I turn to the hall, my heart convulses again.

God, it's really been going through the ringer lately.

"Bri!" I exclaim, moving quickly toward her. Mostly because I'm thrilled she's here, but also because her expression is edgy and it looks like she's about to spin on her heel and get the fuck out.

Considering I was mentally there as well only weeks ago, I hurry over to her before she runs.

"I so glad you're here," I tell her, slowly looping my arm through hers—giving her time to back away, to avoid the contact —before drawing her into the kitchen. "You'll save me from Kathy's instructions on how to properly fold napkins."

"Rude!" Kathy says, not missing a beat and jumping in as exactly as I knew she would. "Just because your mother-in-law wants to make a hundred tiny paper napkin swans—"

Bri chokes, jerks in my hold.

Yup. Definitely ready to run.

Kathy smiles, but holds it together, sighing morosely and saying, "I just wanted something elegant for my daughter-in-law's celebration. No bother." She shrugs. "How about we fold them into flowers instead?"

Bri chokes again.

And Kathy can't hold it together any longer.

Which means that she starts giggling.

And then *I* start giggling because—

"Flowers?" I gasp, loosening my grip on Bri and bending over, holding my middle as I try and stop laughing.

But—

"Your face," I tell Bri, forcing the words out between my guffaws. "Oh, my God, your face." I give myself a moment longer to be amused then, knowing I've pushed it far enough, I manage to get it together and straighten, making introductions. "Bri meet Kathy, Aiden's mom. Her chocolate chip cookies are to die for and her flower organizing skills far outweigh mine. Kathy, this is Bri. She and I share a love for all things romantasy novel related along with a strong dislike for folding napkins into flowers or teeny tiny swans."

Bri was tense when I began talking, but my introduction has her relaxing, her eyes coming to mine for a beat before she looks at Kathy and extends her hand. "It's nice to meet you," she whispers.

"You too, my dear." Kathy wraps her fingers around Bri's. "Now, do you want me to make you a plate so you can get some of my chocolate chip cookies before the grubby hockey players get into them or do you want to help me make those paper flowers?"

"Plate please," Bri and I say at the same time.

Our gazes connect and we grin.

Those smiles widen when Kathy gives an aggrieved sigh.

But when I glance over at her, I see that her eyes are dancing.

Because—instinctively as I knew she would—she's gleaned exactly how much it means that Bri is here.

And—also instinctively—I know that she's found another little duckling to tuck under her wing and never let go.

Which is perfect.

Because Kathy Black is exactly the woman that Bri needs.

I just didn't realize until later that both of us also need a gaggle of grubby hockey players too.

THIRTY-FIVE

Aiden

"THIS PLACE IS SICK!" Smitty booms as I unlock the front door and push it open.

Well, if my mom and Luns needed a warning that I've arrived with a car full of hockey players, here it is.

Gray sighs as he slips by me, toeing off his shoes by the rack and hanging up his coat on the row of hooks I nod toward. "As usual, the man is loud but"—he lowers his voice slightly, as though not wanting to give Smitty more ammunition—"he's also right. This house is amazing."

It really is.

A gorgeous historical craftsman style house with lots of wood trim and enough windows to make it feel bright and sunny rather than shrouded in shadows and darkness.

"What was that?" Smitty shoves his face between us, beard so close that I can see the strands of gray woven through the brown. "I'm right?!" He pumps his fist in the air. "That's right, bitches, I'm *right!*"

"When's Kailey getting here?" I ask Ryan, who's slipped in behind us and closed the door.

"Because she's the only one who can handle him?" he quips.

"Exactly," Gray and I say together.

Smitty's unperturbed (and doesn't deny the statement about his wife *handling* him) as he tells us, "She's finishing up a project"—Kailey is a computer programmer—"but will be here soon."

"Thank God for that," Gray mutters.

"Seriously," I mutter back.

"Rude," Smitty declares then promptly displays exactly how little that bothers him by asking, "Where's the grub?"

Luna steps out into the hall, looking ethereal in a cream shirt and loose-fitting pants, her hair cascading down her shoulders. She's fucking beautiful, and I'm damned glad I've made her mine.

I just need to make sure that *mine* lasts forever.

Because having had her like this...

Nope. I can't ever let her go.

"Is that a gaggle of hockey players I hear?" she says as she comes toward me, and it does my heart good when she moves close, when she lets me wrap an arm around her middle and draw her against me, when she doesn't shy away from me slanting my lips over hers for a short, heated kiss— even in front of the aforementioned *gaggle* of hockey players. She just lightly strokes her fingertips through my beard when I pull back, murmuring, "Hi."

"Hi, tiny tornado."

Her mouth tips up at the edges. "No," she says softly. "That's your mom. She's whipped the house into shape in less time than you'd believe." A beat, her eyes dancing. "How was the flight back?"

Weather meant our intended arrival yesterday had been pushed back to this morning.

"Good," I tell her. "Or good enough to bring said gaggle of rowdy hockey players in my car with more on the way behind me."

"Heaven help us."

"Considering that Smitty's here already..."

"Hey!" he chimes in, right on cue. "Again, *rude!*"

Luna giggles, which is pretty much the worst thing anyone can do when it comes to Smitty—giving him fuel for his incorrigible fire. He perks up, opening his mouth, and considering it's right near my ear, I prepare to put some distance between us, lest the volume tries to ruin my hearing.

Before I can move though, the doorbell rings and my mom zips out into the hall and...

The next ten minutes are chaos.

More guys from the team show up and we're herded from the front door further into the house—Luns wasn't lying, my mom's tornado skills have clearly been on point over the last week.

The place is so gorgeous, it could be a showroom.

There's not a box or speck of dust in sight.

But it doesn't compare to Luna in the space—she shines more brightly than the wood floor, looks more comfortable and at home here than anywhere except when we steal a few minutes for just the two of us in bed or sitting at the kitchen counter, drinking hot cocoa.

There's something settled in her, some rough edge that has been honed down, and that truth sews itself deeply inside me.

My mom has been working her magic.

And Luna is beginning to accept that we're not just a marriage license, not just friends or lovers.

We're *us*.

And one look at her tells me she's getting comfortable with that truth—something that makes me want to preen like a fucking peacock.

I don't have a chance to, though.

Between answering the door and showing my teammates through the house, playing my part of host and newlywed, I'm too busy.

When I finally slip free of my hosting duties, I seek her out in the kitchen. She's filling platters of food on the counter, a teenage girl with brown hair and striking brown eyes—did Bri really come?—hovering close to her side. My mom's close too, as though they're sandwiching the girl, protecting her.

Yup. That definitely must be Bri.

Knowing a bit of what the teenager has been through, I immediately slow my approach, waiting for Luna's eyes connect with mine.

"Hey, sweetheart," I say gently, touching her cheek lightly with the back of my hand.

"All good?" she asks. "We're almost done here."

"All good," I tell her lightly. "The masses have been allowed in to the keep and given the full tour." I snag the empty container from her and bring it over to the sink. "Then, as instructed by the lead tornado"—I hitch my head toward my mom—"they've been sent out back with beers so they don't get underfoot."

"Well done and thanks." A beat, her mouth curving. "From me *and* the lead tornado."

"What's all this tornado talk?" my mom asks in the edgy way she gets when in full party prep mode.

"I used to call Luns tiny tornado because of the way she spun on the ice," I explain without delay—it's best not to delay when my mom is like this. Provide all information. Follow all orders. But teasing? Absolutely not. But have I learned my lesson? I suppose not. Because my next words are, "It also works with a mom in Party Mode."

She scowls at me. "I'm doing this for you, you know."

"I know." I kiss the top of her head, pull her into a half hug. "And I really appreciate it." I take the container she's holding and keep it steady as she finishes with her platter. "I love you, Mom."

Her tongs still.

Then she sets them down and pats my cheek. "I love you too, baby boy."

"I know," I tell her. "And seriously, thank you for all you've done these last few weeks."

"Pish." She waves a hand. "It was nothing."

"It's not nothing," Luna says before I can, coming over and hugging her too. "Thank you for everything, Kathy. I mean it."

My mom sniffs. "Stop it you too."

Probably seeing how close she is to the edge, Luna gives her another hug then releases her, getting back to business. "Take that to the sink," she orders me of another empty container. "Then come meet Bri."

The brunette teenager stiffens for a moment and I know when she exhales and I watch the girl deliberately calm herself, that Luns has called out the introduction in order to give her time to prepare for it.

This girl has been through shit.

And yet...she's here, clearly having stepped out of her comfort zone.

Brave girl.

Strong girl.

A survivor.

Just like my Luns.

I settle the container in the sink then go back over to the trio. "Hey, Bri." I extend my hand slowly. "I'm Aiden."

Her shoulders rise and fall on a slow breath, but she wraps her fingers around mine. "Nice to meet you," she says quietly. Edgily.

I decide to use my previous knowledge and pull out the big guns.

"Did Luna show you the library?"

Her eyes go wide even as Luna's hit mine, sparkling with humor, knowing precisely what I'm doing. "No," she says, nudging my side. "But when things calm down and our social batteries are drained I figured that Bri and I would hide there."

"You have a *library?*" Bri asks, clearly in awe.

"Less library and more room crammed with books since Kathy helped me unpack the boxes. And yes," she adds, bumping Bri's shoulder with her own. "There are loads of books in there that you'll like." A wink. "And that you can borrow."

"Really?"

"Really *really*," Luns teases.

Bri opens her mouth to reply, but the moment is broken by a big, bearded—*loud*—hockey player.

"The entertainment has arrived!" Smitty calls as he bursts into the kitchen holding a huge plastic tub that—heaven help me—appears to contain a karaoke machine. "Who's ready to sing, bitches?!"

Christ.

This is my nightmare.

Especially since Luna loves karaoke.

So, there's definitely going to be video of me on social media dueting some pop ballad.

"Let's fucking go!" Smitty cheers, rattling the box.

"Smitty!" my mom cries. "Language."

"Lang—" He frowns. Then freezes, spotting Bri. "Oh, young ears. My bad."

"Excuse my husband," Kailey says, touching his shoulder as she shifts from behind his bulk and moves toward me. "Aiden, sorry I'm late. It's good to see you again."

"No apologies." I tell her, hugging her quickly. "You figure out the issue with your project?"

"No." She scowls. "There's a bug somewhere, but I needed a break before I sort it out." Her scowl deepens. "*If* I figure it out."

"You'll figure it out, little bird," Smitty murmurs, voice gentled in a way that's special only to Kailey. "You always do."

She touches his jaw, and I watch the big man melt when she lifts up and whispers something in his ear.

I know that Bri sees it too.

Because her expression clouds with confusion.

Then goes carefully blank.

As though she's storing all of this to sort out later.

Before I can think that through, figure out how best to help with that, my mom zips back to tornado duties.

"Smitty, take the karaoke machine outside and set it up. Aiden, your dad just texted me that he and your siblings need help unloading the car. Bri and Luna, you're relieved of duty. Go be social."

Luns and Bri exchange a look—

"And being social means *not* hiding in the library," my mom chides. "It means eating, drinking, and *socializing*."

Their twin scowls at being thwarted has laughter bubbling in my chest.

But before I can let it free, the doorbell rings again.

And...it's back to work.

THIRTY-SIX

Luna

"I WANT IT THAT WAAAAY!"

I wince at the sheer volume of Smitty, even as my amusement wins out.

How does the man know every single line to the boy band classic?

I have no clue...and yet, he's rocking it.

"This makes no sense," Bri says softly.

"What doesn't?" I ask, turning my eyes from the horror show that is Smitty's rendition and glancing over at Bri.

She's scowling. "He's making a fool of himself, and he doesn't care."

My lips twitch as Smitty wraps up the song and tries to pass the mic to Gray—a man who definitely isn't interested in *making a fool of himself* with or without a microphone. When that doesn't work, he hands it over to Ryan, who takes his time selecting a slow rock ballad that has everyone bopping their heads and tapping their feet.

"I think the best part of Smitty—and let me preface this by saying I'm still getting to know him—is that he is unequivocally himself and doesn't care who knows it." A beat. "Kind of like Kathy."

Bri tilts her head to the side, studying him, then turning her head to Kathy, who's relinquished her party prep kingdom in the kitchen and is now sitting in a chair next to Carrie, the two of them cackling about something as they each enjoy a glass of wine.

Bri glances back down at Ryan, who's trying to coax Aiden into taking a turn, taking her time processing my words.

Then she smiles.

It's small, but it's there.

At least until Smitty starts heading our way.

Then her face goes blank and she inches behind me.

Damn.

I hate that for her.

But I don't bring her instinctive action up, just smile at Smitty as he comes over, trying to smooth over any awkwardness.

Despite that, he notices Bri's hesitation, and I watch his entire demeanor change—slowing his pace, gentling his movements, quieting his voice.

Bold and brash become soft and easy.

"You two ladies need anything?" The question doesn't boom. It floats through the air, landing delicately on our ears... and I realize it's kind of how he handles his wife, Kailey—with the utmost care.

Bold and brash and...a big ol' teddy bear.

My heart squeezes.

"No," I tell him, slanting a look at Bri, who shakes her head. "I think we're good."

"Cake? Champagne?" He waggles his brows. "Another

glorious rendition of a Backstreet Boys classic from my glorious vocal cords?"

Bri giggles.

It's quiet, so quiet that I barely hear it.

But, again, it's *there*.

"Don't encourage him," Kailey says as she comes over, loops her arm through Smitty's, and smiles up at him. She's a quiet woman, the polar opposite of Smitty. They shouldn't work but they do.

Probably because he's the aforementioned big ol' teddy bear.

"Encourage?" he asks, affecting outrage. "I am the karaoke *master*. I need no encouragement."

She lifts on tiptoe, presses a kiss to his bearded cheek. "That we all know."

"Rude." He taps the tip of her nose then sweeps a hand out. "Maybe I'll gift you all my vocal talents again."

"You can"—her eyes sparkle with mischief I wouldn't expect from someone so quiet—"but that might make me bust out the wombat song."

The big man rears back, face going pale. "You wouldn't dare."

"You know me. You love me." A beat, those mischief-laden eyes holding his. "So yeah, what do you think?"

"No more Backstreet Boys."

Another kiss on his cheek, this one a loud smack. "Exactly."

Bri giggles. And, God, I love that sound.

"What's scary about wombats?" she whispers to me.

But, Smitty, with all of his superpowers, hears. "What's *scary* about wombats?" he asks, shuddering. "First of all, it's the beady little eyes. They're dark like death and pierce straight into your soul, reminding you of the fragility of the human condition—"

Kailey groans, head dropping back, gaze on the sky. "Here we go."

"And there are the claws—"

"Luns."

I turn away from Smitty as he starts talking about cube-shaped poo and see that Aiden is behind me with two men I don't recognize, though both look relatively familiar. As though I've seen them somewhere before.

More hockey people, maybe.

"Hey, tiny tornado," he murmurs, bending so the words are spoken directly into my ear. "I invited someone."

"And I likely overstepped because I invited someone else," the older of the two men says, his gentle blue eyes coming to mine. "I hope you don't mind a couple of party crashers."

"Of course not," I say, though I think my uncertainty shines out through my words because when he extends his hand, his voice is careful. "I'm Jean-Michel."

Another blip of familiarity, but I still can't place the men. "I'm Luna," I say. "It's, uh, nice to meet you."

He releases my hand, glances around. "Your house is beautiful."

"It was my grandmother's."

"I know." His eyes sparkle with something I can't comprehend, other than it seems like he's in on a joke that I don't know yet.

"Jean-Michel is Jean-Michel *Dubois*," Aiden says. "Owner of the Eagles and also—"

"Titan Capital," I whisper.

Holy shit.

There are people like my family, who—my restricted access to the family trust fund aside—have money to live comfortably and somewhat lavishly. And then there are people like Jean-Michel.

He could buy this house.

Buy the neighborhood.

Hell, buy the entire city and it wouldn't even create a dent in his coffers.

And he's standing in Grams's back yard.

Thank God Kathy helped me put up the twinkly lights.

"Aiden told me a little about what's been going on with your family—"

My eyes go wide, hope blooming in my belly. This man could take on my brother and father, could truly help me make a difference.

"—and also some about your dreams for Smythe—"

My eyes go wider, hope growing, spreading.

"—and while I don't know a ton about medical products—"

My stomach sinks, the hope that had been building inside me deflating like a leaking balloon.

But he's still talking. "Luckily, Jace does."

Jean-Michel nods at the man next to him, tall and handsome with a kind smile.

He sticks his hand out. "Jace Henderson. I own Genencore."

My mouth drops open and I robotically shake Jace's hand, but I'm looking Aiden. With complete and utter shock.

Because...

If Jean-Michel is a titan—no pun intended—in the business world, Jace is renowned in the biomedical sphere...*and* for his work in making health care accessible to everyone.

And Aiden did this for me.

Brought these men into my orbit.

Slowly, I turn to face him, mouth opening, all the feelings I have for this him—the boy I knew and loved, the man I'm still learning but absolutely loving now—welling up, prepared to enter the air.

But I don't get that far, don't get to give voice to the words.

Because I hear—

"You fucking bitch!"

And turn just in time to see my brother and father barreling through the back door of Gram's house.

The karaoke—a rendition of *Don't Stop Believing*—cuts off.

The yard goes quiet as everyone turns to see what the commotion is.

And I feel my temper snap.

This again.

This a-fucking-*gain*.

Why do they have to keep coming into my life and messing up beautiful moments?

Why do they have to keep trying to control me?

Why do they have to keep ruining my life?

But before I can let any of *that* loose—

I see a flash of brown hair as Aiden tucks me behind him, protecting me, not knowing I'm ready to breathe fire.

"Don't call her that!" Bri shouts, rushing in front of us, in front of Jean-Michel and Jace.

She puts her arms out to block my brother and father from proceeding.

But they don't care—about women, about people they think are below them, about anyone other than themselves and their wallets.

My dad lifts a hand...

And shoves her.

And the entire yard goes deadly quiet.

THIRTY-SEVEN

Aiden

THE FIRST ONE TO get there is Gray.

He crouches down and hesitates when Bri flinches before he murmurs something.

A long heartbeat passes before she nods and he carefully helps her up to her feet, tucking her behind his big body.

The music has cut out and pride flickers through me when I see that every single one of my teammates who are here today is standing, silently staring down Luna's brother and father, murder emanating out of their bodies, filling the air with tension strung so tightly, one tiny spark is all it will take to set it alight.

All at once, Frank and John seem to realize that they're in danger.

Critical danger.

Frank's eyes go wide, and he steps back, halfway shielding himself behind his son.

Fucking coward.

"Who the fuck is that?" I hear Jean-Michel growl, and if murder is the name of the game in Luna's gorgeous, flower-filled-huge-oak-tree-shaded back yard with twinkly lights my mom had my dad and me stringing over the last week, Jean-Michel's tone is somehow even more deadly.

It speaks of kings who'll decapitate, who'll give the order for drawing and quartering, who'll display bodies from city walls, and who'll do it with enjoyment.

With fucking *vigor*.

"That is Frank Maybelle, CEO of Smythe Industries," Jace says quietly, his anger frigid cold, so chilled it'll blacken skin, burning flesh with its frost. "And his useless piece of shit son, John."

Jean-Michel's eyes come to mine.

And I know the short conversation I had with him the other night was the best thing I could have done.

He might have been in before.

But now he's fucking *in*.

Victory ricochets through my insides, knowing that this shit's going to get taken care of, that Luna won't have to deal with it, with *them* any longer, but even as I'm tabling that emotion, preparing to show these fuckers the door, Luna—as usual—surprises me.

Not by showing strength.

She's always had a steel spine, an intense work ethic, strong ideals...but sometimes those have been overshadowed by etiquette and her brother and father's overbearing nature.

She would roll her eyes, let them vent their bullshit, and then quietly go the direction she wanted.

That was the way of Grams, so it's not a surprise.

But that's not the way of Luna, not today.

"You need to leave," she says, slipping from my grip and stepping forward, out of my reach, out of my protection.

Heart pulsing, I follow her, but she's moving fast, marching forward at a far quicker clip than I anticipated.

She pauses by Bri, looking into the girl's face for a heartbeat, but whatever she sees there must be reassuring because she just nods sharply then keeps on marching.

Not stopping until she's a foot away from her brother.

John, dumbass that he is, underestimates her as usual, sneering as she halts in front of him. "Oh," he drawls. "I'm sorry. Are we interrupting your little party for corporate fraud? Fake weddings don't need parties to celebrate them, so I'm sure you'll survive."

"There's nothing fake about Aiden and me," she says and my heart spasms, love for this woman filling every cell in my body. "Although—"

Another spasm, this time fierce and painful.

Is she going to tell everyone the truth like she told my mom? That it's complicated and means something, but not what they think?

Or worse, is she going to tell them that this *is* fake and meaningless and that it *is* strictly business, that I'm a dumb fuck who fell in love when I was really supposed to be fixing things and—

"—if you two hadn't been such pushy assholes"—she turns to Bri and winces—"sorry for the language—"

I hear a quiet chuckle, see that Jean-Michel has flanked me, Jace next to him, my teammates at my side. And my family is right here too, Carrie and her husband Dave and Ralph, and my parents, my mom having tucked Bri against her.

Fuck.

That hits hard.

In the best possible way.

"I curse all the time," Bri says, making Luns smile for a fleeting moment before she focuses her fierce glare back on her brother. "If it wasn't for you two, I never would have searched Aiden out again." Her shoulders tense, gaze coming to mine. "I was too scared I would end up like all the other Maybelle women—alone and sad and wishing I'd never put my hand near the stove, so I wouldn't have gotten burned."

"I think alone and sad are your destiny," John says. "And hopefully, with third-degree burns because you're such a pain in the ass."

Gray curses softly, takes a step forward, but Smitty snags his shoulder, shakes his head.

Rightly reading that Luna needs this moment.

To come into her own.

To say her piece.

To protect *herself*.

More spasms clench my heart—both because I'm shoving away flashes of a future without this woman passing through my mind like a depressing slideshow and also because—

"No," she says, turning and looking at me, her eyes so bright and beautiful when they connect with mine that my lungs freeze, not restarting until she glances at the semi-circle of people surrounding her.

"No," she says again. "I'm not alone." Her chin lifts. "All that's left of my family may be jerks, but I'm building a new one—and they don't get sick satisfaction from hurting or manipulating or trying to squeeze every bit of usefulness out of me. They like me as I am, and they have my back instead of sucking me dry."

Christ. My throat is tight.

My eyes burn.

Because I'm so damned proud of her.

How had I ever let her go a decade ago?

Of course, I know why.

Youth and time, busy lives and heavy travel, spending too much time being an idiot while working toward my dreams.

And...immaturity—not understanding exactly how precious of a gift she is.

Lucky for me, she *did* knock on my door.

Because I recognize the treasure, the beauty of her, and I'm prepared to fight tooth and nail for it.

Today.

Forever.

"See," she says, "you chipped away at me when I was a girl, wore me down when I was caring for Grams. You took advantage of my grief, and you poked and prodded and eroded anything I wanted to do with Smythe, no matter how good. And for a while, I believed it was better to back down, to walk away. Then Aiden helped me fight—"

"Fuck yeah, sweetheart," Smitty says.

Luns glances back at him, a soft smile on her face, before she's turning back, stepping closer. "The thing is, you pushed me too far. Now, I'm *not* alone, I'm not bereft with grief, and I'm sure as hell not uncertain and cowed. Oh no"—a shake of her head—"I'm finally thinking clearly. And I'm going to fight for what I want—even if that means going toe-to-toe with you."

Frank Maybelle looks rightfully terrified.

But John—never the smartest tool in the box—doesn't seem to realize the end is near. His sneer grows at Luna's words, deepening the ugly furrows in his face. "Such idiotic sentiments." A sniff. "Especially when we can draw this out, can bankrupt you in a legal battle that will go on for years."

"And drain the family's trust fund when my lawyers come after it for fees?" she asks archly.

Fuck yeah, sweetheart is right.

John growls, steps forward, lifting his hand as though he's going to hit her.

I move without thinking, darting between them, and grabbing him by the throat, squeezing.

Tightly.

John chokes, his face turning purple, and he scrabbles at my hand, trying to pull my fingers free.

But, yeah, that's not going to fucking happen. "You fucking touch her," I growl, holding his eyes that are the same color as Luna's eyes and yet nothing alike, "and I will rip you apart, piece by piece by—" I shake him like a rag doll. "—*piece.*"

He gargles out something unintelligible.

But I don't loosen my grip enough to discern it.

"Do you get me?" I grit out and because it feels so good to put the fucker in his place, I shake him again. "Do *you* get me?"

A bobbing nod, even as the purple shade of his face darkens, as he scrabbles at my hand.

"Aiden," Luna murmurs, lightly touching my arm. "Honey, it's okay—"

I glance at her then shake John again. "It's not fucking *okay* for him to do this shit to you. He's hurt you. He's put you through hell. He fucking pushed Bri"—I see Bri twitch out of the corner of my eyes, but I'm too busy choking John to look at her—"and he was going to *hit* you—"

"Honey." Her hand slides to mine, gently tugging at my fingers, silently encouraging me to let go. "I've got this."

I suck in a breath, striving for control.

I don't find it.

I still have to force myself to loosen my fingers slowly, one by one, to step back, and I can't stop myself from staring him down as I say, "Touch her again and I will fucking *end* you."

"I will fucking sue you," he rasps out, clutching at his throat.

"We have a dozen witnesses for your assault on a minor," I say. "You really want to play that game?"

Luna laces her fingers with mine, squeezes, and I take the cue to shut the fuck up.

My palms still itch to hit him, but my woman is in complete control as she says, "You were right, I don't want the dirty money. And I don't need it. I have Gram's place and I have good people taking my back like Aiden and Kathy and Mike—"

"And me."

My eyes skim to the right, seeing that Smitty's come up, flanking her other side.

"And I have Smitty," she murmurs, face softening slightly when she looks at my teammate.

"And me," Gray says.

"And Gray." Her throat works.

"And me," Bri says, stepping out of the circle of my mom's arm, her shoulders ramrod straight.

"And you have me," Ryan says.

"And Ryan."

"Not to jump in on this whole *I am Spartacus* thing," Jace says. "But you also have me."

Frank pales, terror growing, clearly recognizing the billionaire biomedical tycoon.

But it's what his expression does when Jean-Michel chimes in, "And me," that truly warms my heart.

Luna is compassion and kindness, strength and life...but her father only respects money and power and...

Fear.

And Jean-Michel can evoke that in spades.

I grin, no longer wanting to commit murder.

If I'm in jail, I won't get to see the pain he dishes out to the Maybelle assholes.

"And Jean-Michel Dubois and Jace Henderson," Luna tells them, her chin lifting higher. "So, yes, we can absolutely take this battle to court. We can draw it out for years and years and *years.*" Her tone hardens. "But I'm not going to give up. And because of that, I'm going to win." She glances up at me. "Because how can't I with all of these great people at my side?"

God, I love this woman.

"Let's go," Frank says, tugging at John's arm.

He shakes off his father. "No, I need—"

"No," Frank snaps. "We *need* to go."

"Yes," I say, stepping forward again, Smitty and Gray right beside me. "You need to go."

John tries to stare me down.

Newsflash, that doesn't fucking work.

So when Frank tugs at his arm again, he finally gives up the bravado and turns, following his father through the doors and back into the house.

"I'll just make sure they leave," Gray tells me quietly, his words still filled with deadly intent.

Not trusting myself to see to that—*and* keep my hands to myself—I nod. "Thanks."

He nods back and it's curt.

Then he follows them into the house, Smitty and Ryan on his heels.

I touch Luna's cheek before our family closes ranks around us. "You okay, my tiny tornado?" I ask before we're interrupted, needing the assurance from her before we deal with explanations and reassurances and...with all that's my parents and siblings and teammates and...her newfound billionaire fairy godfathers.

"I'm okay." Her lips kick up and when I open my mouth, she presses a finger to it, saying, "Because I have all of this." She sweeps her hand around the party, everyone already doing their best to get over the interruption and back to the festivities.

Ryan has come back outside and is passing out beers, my mom has Bri tucked close to her side again and is making her laugh, and Smitty...well, he waltzes out, gray on his heels, and loops his arm through my woman's, dragging her to the makeshift stage and tempting her into a duet.

When I was traded to the Grizzlies from the Breakers, I didn't know what my hockey future would look like.

The family I found in Baltimore was unique, special, impossible to create anywhere else—

The music cranks on to an ear-piercing volume and I wince.

Then shake my head as Smitty and Luna begin belting out a boy band ballad.

But I do it smiling.

Because it turns out that if I find the right people, I can build a family that's just as good here.

That's maybe—somehow—even better I think as I look to Luna, who's been drawn into singing, who's already shaking off the bitterness of her family, her brightness shining through the huge smile on her face.

She's fucking incredible, fucking *perfect*.

Jean-Michel pats my shoulder and I manage to tear my gaze away from the beauty of my woman to see his eyes shining just as bright—only not with beauty.

With brutal challenge.

Like he can't wait for the confrontation ahead.

"Oh, Aiden," he says, clapping me on the shoulder again then jerking his chin at Jace, who nods back, his expression just as fierce, "I'm so glad we talked."

He's glad?

That whole scene was a fucking shit show.

And I *still* want to pummel someone.

"You are?" I mutter.

He drops his hand to his side. "Yup." A beat. "Because now it's fucking *on*."

THIRTY-EIGHT

Luna

"DID YOU HAVE THE BOARD MEETING?"

I smile at Bri as I walk into the common space. As usual, she has a book in her lap, but she is also more animated than I've ever seen her, her confidence growing daily since she showed up at the party for Aiden and me.

"We did," I say, sitting down across from her and nudging her foot with mine.

She looks rested and calm—and I know it's partly because she accepted the bakery job and the bed here at the shelter.

But I know the rest of it is Kathy.

And Smitty.

And Gray.

And Ryan and Aiden and all the rest of the Blacks.

They've hovered, checking in, reminding her that she's not alone, showing her that there are good people in the world—connection without pushing.

Well, there was Kathy offering Bri a spot in her guest bedroom.

But she didn't protest—much—when Bri declined, something my little teenage sidekick also did of Aiden's and my offer to stay with us at Gram's place.

My place.

It still feels weird to say that.

Same as it feels weird to say I'm married.

And that I'm the majority shareholder of Smythe Industries.

I grin.

"Well?" she demands.

"Well...we had the meeting."

"Yes"—she makes a hurry up sign with her hand—"and what happened at that meeting?"

I shrug, affecting casual when I'm anything but in this moment. "It turns out that joining a partnership with Genencore"—Jace Henderson's company—"and Titan Capital"—Jean-Michel's firm—"calmed the board enough that they voted in favor of my insulin program."

Her eyes light up. "Really?"

I nod. "Really."

It was almost anticlimactic, how the pieces fell in place after Jean-Michel and Jace joined my side, and— if I'm being honest—I'm a little disappointed. I finally found the strength to fight...and then I didn't need to.

Not much anyway.

Still, I'm sure that time will come eventually.

Because my brother and father have lost a battle, but they're not the type to give up on the war.

Lucky, I have smart, capable people on my side.

Like Jean-Michel and Jace putting their heads together and somehow a few stories got "leaked" (and yes, I'm making mental air quotes at that word) about what our future plans for growth at Smythe are, causing the stock prices to go up.

So, the shareholders were happy.

Which means the board was happy coming in to the meeting today.

And because I am now the majority owner of Smythe on said board, the others have an interest in keeping me happy... and ignoring my brother and father's blustering.

New projects with Genen-core and capital from Titan along with a positive news cycle?

It's like the businessman's trifecta of orgasm material.

"That's awesome!" she exclaims. "You did it!"

"The legal fight is far from over," I feel obligated to remind her.

And myself.

Because...stubborn Maybelles.

"Smitty says that JM"—a moniker I've learned that Jean-Michel isn't entirely fond of, but he tolerates...probably because he figures there's no point in doing anything *but* tolerating Smitty's nonsense and maybe also because Bri has picked it up and the grumpy billionaire has a soft spot for her—"has really good lawyers."

"He does," I agree.

"So"—she shrugs—"that's that. It'll all work out."

I still.

Because where the hell has this girl been? It'll all work out? And that's not just lip service—I can see she believes that. It's in her eyes, her smile, her words.

And why do I feel the same?

The magic of Aiden and company.

Of love and connection and...

Two tenacious billionaires.

I nudge her foot with mine again. "That's it," I agree with a nod. "It'll all work out."

Teenage curiosity suitably satisfied, she picks up a book and tosses it into my lap. "Angie"—one of the other girls who lives permanently at the shelter—"recommended this. Do you want to read it together?"

"Is it fantasy?" I ask.

Her mouth kicks up. "Yes."

"Does it have sexy fae heroes?"

"Yup."

"And a kickass heroine?"

"Absolutely."

I clutch the book to my chest. "Then I am so *absolutely* in."

She holds up another copy, mouth turning up. "I knew you would be."

"Right, then," I say, settling back in the chair opposite her. "How about one chapter before I have to head out?"

"Just *one* chapter," she agrees, opening to the first page.

Spoiler alert: we don't read just one chapter.

And also...

Despite my earlier certainty, it doesn't all work out.

Not by a long shot.

So, one chapter turned into five chapters and pretty soon we were a quarter of the way through the book.

"Angie was right," I tell Bri as I force myself to close the book, gather up my things, and stand. "This is really good."

"And there are four more in the series," she says and it's so nice to see her smiling.

"Well I know I'm not going to get anything done for the next week."

"Hey"—she closes her own book and stands, trailing me to the door—"binge-reading an entire series isn't nothing."

"I like the way you think." Hitching my purse over my shoulder, we pause at the door that leads to the sleeping quarters of the shelter. "Will I see you tomorrow at Kathy's for dinner?"

She nods. "She's teaching me how to make chocolate chip cookies."

My stomach rumbles and we both laugh. "Well, clearly, I can't wait to taste the results." I dare to bump her shoulder with mine, joy in my heart when she bumps me back. I know that, for as comfortable as she's gotten with Kathy, physical contact is still tough for her, so don't want to push it. "Goodnight, sweetheart," I murmur.

"'Night," she murmurs back but before I can leave, she says, "Luns?"

I pause with my hand on the metal bar that opens the door, glance back over my shoulder. "Yeah, honey?"

She doesn't say anything but moves in a rush, closing the distance between us in a second, so fast I don't have a chance to brace or get out of her way.

And it's a good thing.

Bracing would do nothing—because the impact isn't physical.

And getting out the way would have been a huge mistake—because I would have missed *this*.

Her arms wrapping around me and squeezing tight as she gives me the best hug of my life.

And I've had some pretty great hugs in my life.

"Thanks," she whispers after a long moment and I know it's not for reading with her tonight or even for the invite to the party that brought her into the Grizzlies and Black fold. It's for everything—being here, being a person she can trust, showing her there's more to life than just surviving, that we can fight and laugh and *live*.

And along the way, I've learned the very same lessons.

Learned so much more.

Because I remembered what it felt like to be loved—and how to give that love to the right people.

But I don't say any of that.

Not tonight.

Sappy exchanges can come another night.

I just hug her back just as tightly and say, "you're welcome."

And I don't let go until she does.

Then with the hug held close to my heart, I say goodbye, get into my car, and I drive home.

Unfortunately, what I find there isn't a big, bearded hockey player whose heart is mine...

Instead, I stumble onto my worst nightmare.

THIRTY-NINE

Aiden

I FROWN as I look at my phone, something prickling at back of my nape.

"What is it?" Smitty says.

"Nothing," I mutter, shoving my phone away and going back to getting undressed.

"Dude."

"What?" I ask as I yank at my laces, shove off my skates.

"That's not the face of a man who's thinking about *nothing*." He tosses his jersey into the bin in the center of the room. "You played great tonight, so it's not hockey." He slants his gaze in my direction. "Did you fuck up with Luna and need to apologize? I figured you'd have a longer grace period considering the whole aligning your wife with some powerful billionaires thing, but who am I to know?" He lifts one big shoulder then drops it. "I suggest flowers and chocolate and maybe a brand-new laptop."

"What?" I grumble. "No jewelry?"

"My woman would rather have computer parts," he says. "So, no. I can't vouch for the apologetic properties of jewelry."

I roll my eyes.

Still, Luns loved the ring I bought her, so I think I might have better luck with jewelry than Smitty does.

But the apologetic property of diamonds are honestly the least of my concerns right now.

Because I texted Luna before the game.

And she still hasn't replied.

Not that I expect her to respond to me instantly—but it's been four hours.

And my nape is prickling.

And...

"What's it for Luna?" he asks and I blink, putting my phone aside again.

"What?"

"Aside from chocolate and flowers, what's Luna's soft spot?"

Books.

My mouth kicks up.

And ice cream.

And jewelry.

"You're not going to share?"

"Nah." I yank off my socks, my shin guards, then make short work of the rest of my gear.

"Lame," he grumbles. But he's smiling, and I know he's not upset when he says, "Think your mom is due for another round of karaoke yet?"

God, no.

I shudder.

"Nope."

"No?"

"She pulled a muscle in that dance-off with you at the party, remember?"

"I told her she needed to go easy on the splits."

My mother and Smitty together are a dangerous proposition.

I shake my head and add, knowing I need to give him shit... because this is a hockey locker room and things don't feel right without dishing up shit—even with my mind prickling, worry snaking through my stomach. "And also no more karaoke because my ears can't handle another round." I strip off my jock, my long-sleeved Grizzlies-emblazoned undershirt, toss the latter into the dirty pile, hang the former with the rest of my equipment so it can be cleaned (well, everything except for my lucky socks, that is).

"Rude," Smitty mutters, glaring at me as I snag a towel and head into the showers.

But I make it quick because the conversation with Smitty is semi-humorous as always, but it doesn't change the niggling in the back of my mind and I don't want to delay further.

Luna didn't text back.

From the moment she leveled with me about everything, she's always texted back, always been available.

It's been easy, in fact—falling back into the old routine, becoming partners in crime again.

Turns out when you're hopping into a fake marriage with both parties aware of exactly what's at stake, the bullshit falls away.

And we can just be *us*.

It also helps that we set the sheets on fire.

Orgasms. Right.

Smitty buys computer parts...I'll win over my woman with orgasms.

And jewelry. And pastries. And ice cream. And books.

I rush through drying off and getting dressed, knowing that since it's after eleven, I know exactly which one of those I can utilize tonight if I really *did* piss off Luns tonight.

That would be...orgasms.

Win-win.

And yeah, maybe Smitty *is* on to something.

I snag my stuff, hurry to my car, and head home, glad we're playing in San Jose and not on the road, so it doesn't take long to make the drive. The lights are blazing when I pull into the driveway, something that intensifies the niggling in my mind, especially when I spot an unfamiliar car parked in front of the house.

The board meeting was today.

Luns got her victory.

And her brother and father—

"Shit," I hiss as I pull to a halt, slamming the transmission into park. I throw open the door and don't think, just haul ass inside.

Shouting reaches me the second I shove into the mudroom, angry voices echoing down the hall.

I rush forward, skidding as I turn the corner into the kitchen, temper spiking when I see Luna arching away from her brother, whose face is mottled red and scrunched up in anger...and shoved right into Luna's.

"What did I fucking say?" I growl, striding forward and grabbing John's shirt, ripping him away from my woman.

He stumbles back, falling hard into the cabinets.

"I-I tried to stop him."

I spin, realize that I missed the other person in the room.

The other *man*.

Or the one pretending to be a man, anyway.

"You tried to stop him?" I grit out, striding toward Frank Maybelle, glaring at her father. "You fucking *tried?*"

MARRIED TO NUMBER 22   249

"Aiden—"

My eyes slice to Luna's—and whatever she sees in my gaze has her lips clamping together, swallowing down the rest of the sentence. What I see in hers, however, has my temper ratcheting up.

Fear.

Of me.

Grinding my teeth together, I swivel my gaze back toward Frank. "You tried to stop him?" I ask icily.

A nod that's so rapid and uncontrolled, he resembles a bobblehead. "Yes," he says. "Our team of lawyers has advised that we keep our distance considering the legal fight ahead, but John's always been a little bit of a..."

"An asshole?" I supply.

"Impulsive," Frank says quietly as John groans and pushes to his feet.

"Aiden!"

I jerk at Luna's warning, turning just in time to see John launch himself at me, proving that impulsivity—and frankly, his stupidity—all over again.

I sidestep him, wince when he bounces off the cabinets a second time.

"You know," I say, nudging him back with my foot when he swipes at my leg, "you could always find a way to work with Luna—do some good as you take advantage of capitalism and all that."

"The board would never agree—" Frank begins.

"Except, they did," Luna reminds him.

"Yeah, because of Henderson and Dubois," John snaps. "They're like the golden stepchild mafia—they always get their way and the press eats that shit up."

"Because they're trying to do good things," Luna says, coming to my side, leaning against me, soothing the rough edges of my guilt twining through my insides because I scared her. "Like what I want to do."

"Good things that will bankrupt us," John sneers.

"No." She sighs. "But you've never trusted anyone but yourself so what's the point of trying to convince you? Jace and Jean-Michel are on my side, I have Grams's stock and the majority shares *and* the board on my side. You're out of moves, John, so you can either get with the program or you can get left behind."

"You—"

"And that's the last thing I'm going to say about it," she says. Her voice is like steel and fuck, but I'm so damned proud of her. "If you have a problem with that then I don't know what to tell you except that the next time you show up unwelcome and get in my face, I'll be skipping the side of intimidation you're attempting to dish out and go straight to calling the police."

"I'll give you your share of the trust fund." Desperate words.

Pathetic words.

Even Frank, the coward now trying to make himself disappear into the cabinets, winces.

"You mean the share I'm going to have anyway?" she asks archly.

He scowls.

And it's late, I came home to my woman dealing with her asshole family—*again*—and I'm beyond done with this shit.

"Consider our first call in the morning to be arranging for a restraining order," I tell him.

That scowl deepens.

"And that's your cue to leave," Luns says.

So calmly. So cooly. So collected that we may as well be ordering pastries at Molly's.

God, I love her.

"Like now," I mutter, striding to the front door and pulling it open. Then glaring at them before they move my way...and then out onto the porch.

I slam the door, twist the lock.

"Thank God they're go—*ack!*"

I crush her against my chest, absorbing her squeak. "Fuck, tiny tornado, you scared the shit out of me."

She frowns. "What? How?"

"You didn't text me back and then I came in to *that* shit again." I tuck her hair behind her ear. "I thought you were pissed at me, not getting accosted by your fucking family again."

"I think that maybe I need to work with Jean-Michel's security company," she says when I finally loosen my grip.

"You're right," I say softly. "*We* do."

Her face gentles. "You thought I didn't answer your text because I was mad?"

I nod.

She winces, chagrin in those beautiful eyes. "Bri brought me a book for a read along." A wince. "We got a little... distracted by the sexy fae prince, and I lost track of time."

I start laughing.

"What?"

I take her hand, draw her with me out into the garage, pulling my bag from the back seat. Then the bag from inside that. "A sexy fae prince like this one?"

"What is this?" she asks quietly.

"A book I picked up for you earlier this week...and was going to bribe you with tonight if you were pissed at me."

Her brow furrows. "How could I have been pissed at you?"

I shrug. "Because women are confusing?" A beat. "And

maybe also because I was hoping this and a bevy of orgasms would make you *un*pissed?"

She giggles.

Then lightly touches my cheek. "I didn't even have a chance to make you your hot cocoa."

"Trust me," I tell her, "orgasms are better. Plus," I murmur, peeling her hand from my cheek and pressing a kiss to her palm, "holding you as I drift off is the best sleep aid on the planet."

I expect her to laugh.

Or to swat at my chest.

But, as usual, my tiny tornado surprises me...

By bursting into tears.

"I...Luns, sweetheart, what's the matter?"

She lifts her head, sobs still hitching her chest, tears streaming down her cheeks. "I-it's j-just—" A deep, shaky breath. "I love you so damned much!"

FORTY

Luna

"WHAT'S THAT, SWEETHEART?" he says quietly, smoothing back my hair, sounding completely befuddled.

And I get why.

Because I've lost my mind.

Despite everything, I still want to clamp my hand over my mouth, to smother those words.

The curse is...well, it's going to wreak havoc on this moment and ruin my life with Aiden and I'll be alone and sad and—

Just stop being so fucking afraid.

Just cut the bullshit.

Just accept the truth I know in my heart.

Of course there's no curse.

There's tragedy and there's life and there's happiness and there are beautiful moments punctuated by sadness and grief and *love.*

So much damned love that it seems to grow by the moment.

And God—

What have I learned since I knocked on Aiden's door? That there's so much more to be gained by living than sitting on the sidelines and hiding from real connection.

Plus, who am I kidding?

Even when I felt alone, I still had Grams and her house, Bri and my job at the shelter, and the moment I saw Aiden on TV, I did everything in my power to search him out.

To tie myself to him.

And Kathy and Matt and Smitty and the others.

I could have walked away from Smythe, could have sold Grams's house and started a simple life over somewhere else. I could have contented myself with doing something good that I could accomplish on my own.

But...as Grams knew, I wouldn't walk away.

I would fight.

I would find a way.

Like she had. Like my mom had. Like every woman in my family had.

I always thought the endings were a tragedy, that damned curse was a millstone I couldn't shed, but the real tragedy was thinking that a life well-lived isn't worth it just because the ending didn't turn out as planned.

It was easier to think that I didn't *deserve* a happy ending.

Wasn't worthy of it because—

Why?

My family's curse?

My father's words?

My brother's bullying?

Or fear and my own insecurities?

Because Aiden...he's different.

He's *mine*.

Maybe this marriage won't work out, maybe I'll end up

alone in a year or five or ten, but I'm not going to let this gift go —not going to squander the gift of *him*, of living a life that's bright and exciting, vast and challenging, just because I'm scared to fail, scared to be hurt, scared to be alone.

When I was learning to skate, I was afraid to fall.

But I pushed through the bruised knees to excel.

When I was learning to jump, I worried about the landings.

But what I remember the most now is the exultation of completing my first axel.

When I was falling for Aiden as a teenager, I feared I'd hold him back from his dreams.

But the moment I saw him again on TV I was so damned proud of all he accomplished.

When I was caring for Grams, I was scared that every moment with her would be the last.

But each story, each hug, each time I held her hand was a gift.

And when I lost her, almost lost her house, thought that my program at Smythe would never happen...I wasn't fearful.

Instead, I was determined.

To make her memory count.

To figure out how to keep her house.

To find a way to gain control of those shares and make my program happen.

Determined enough to track Aiden down and marry him.

And with all that determination under my belt, me keeping him at a distance—physical or emotional or otherwise—in order to keep my heart safe, barely even crossed my mind.

Because he's Aiden.

The man holding me tightly in his arms and laughing with me over hot chocolate. The man coming to my rescue and consistently putting himself between me and my father, my brother. The man who kissed me gently and passionately in equal measure, who learned my body and has never failed to put my pleasure first. The man who brought me a karaoke-loving hockey player and a pair of billionaires with golden hearts...and the man who's holding me again now, his eyes gentle and patient.

Waiting for me to look at him.

To talk to him.

He touches the backs of his knuckles to my cheek. "You love me?"

I nod and give *him* this gift, this piece of me, knowing he needs it, knowing its beauty is what brings us closer together. Not because I'm trying to pay him back or make up for him helping me...

Because our love isn't a barter system.

It's unquantifiable...and the best freaking feeling in the world.

So, how can I deny him that?

"I think I've loved you from the first time we shared a pretzel together at the rink," I say, covering his hand with mine, soul swelling with joy when he smiles at the memory.

"Because I gave you the bigger half?" he teases.

"Because that was when you first showed me your heart." I settle my hand over his chest. "Showed me how pure and good it is."

"Luns," he murmurs, face going serious. "I've been wanting to tell you I love you since you walked back into my life."

My pulse speeds, but it's not relief I'm feeling.

I already know he loves me—because he's done nothing but show that love to me, over and over again.

"I know you do," I tell him softly.

His expression is gentle as his fingers flex on my cheek. "I love you, my tiny tornado. You clear all the unnecessary nonsense out of my life and leave nothing but clear blue skies in your wake."

"I love *you*." I shift closer. "And this big, beautiful heart that lets you take a chance on a woman who brings storm clouds and thunderstorms into your life that you manage to ward off without even an umbrella."

His green eyes swim with emotion.

And I'm staring at him through watery lenses too. But I don't want to cry. I want to celebrate and I want to drink hot cocoa and I want to fall into bed with this man and kiss every inch of his body.

So, I don't let the tears fall.

Instead, I take his hand, draw him over to the stool, and I say, "And now I think we've surpassed our weather analogies for the night, don't you?"

He grins, draws me into the vee of his legs. "I never know what you're going to say, Luns." He tucks a strand of my hair behind my ear. "And that's one of the many, *many* things I love about you, sweetheart."

"It's Hot chocolate time," I whisper, mostly so I don't cry.

"That'll come later," he says, rising to his feet at the same time as he hefts me up, tossing me over his shoulder. "First, I want to kiss my woman."

"Kind of hard to kiss me in this position," I tell him...or rather, I tell his lush, yummy, bounce-a-quarter-off-of hockey player's ass.

He laughs but keeps pounding up the stairs. "I don't want to kiss your lips. Or at least not those ones," he says with a wicked grin. Something I see because he's hefted me again, dropping me onto the mattress and climbing over the top of me.

"Funny," I say, reaching for the waistband of my pants, "I was thinking the same thing about you."

A searing look as he starts to strip me naked. "That's why

you're perfect," he murmurs. "And mine." He yanks off my pants, nips at the indent of my waist. "And also why I'm never letting you go."

He kisses me, long and slow and deep...and eventually, on both sets of lips. *Heh.*

But through that gloriousness, I manage to say what's in *my* heart too.

"Because I give you blow jobs?" I tease him breathlessly as guides me through an orgasm, quickly starts sending me up the edge for another.

He pauses, head lifting, eyes coming to mine.

And I get the best gift of all.

His laughter...

And then the redoubled efforts of his supremely skilled tongue.

"Later, tiny tornado. The blow job can come later."

EPILOGUE

Aiden, One Year Later

I CHECK the mailbox on my way into the house, knowing that Luna will have forgotten it.

Mostly because she's had a lot of other things on her mind with the rollout of her insulin program over the last couple of weeks.

But also making sure that Bri's felt at home.

Because Bri has finally given in and agreed to move into the Maybelle-Black residence.

She's spent the last year completing her GED, working at the bakery, and...learning to trust the good people around her. And now that she's officially eighteen, she's officially moving in.

Officially letting *us* in.

Well, it was either that or my mom was going to find a way to get her to move there, and that would really cut in on hers and Luns's reading time.

But seriously, she's doing great—making friends, excelling at work and school, and she's even applied to a few colleges for the spring semester, though she's not entirely sure what she wants to study.

Luna thinks that she'll be an author.

And I don't think she's wrong.

I just know that after all that Bri's survived, she can do anything she puts her mind too.

The mailbox is empty except for a few letters, so I snag those, grab the rest of my stuff from the back seat of my car, and head into the house, wondering how I'm going to give Luna her surprise now that we have with a teenager living with us.

No more stair sex.

Or kitchen sex.

Or living room sex.

Definitely no library sex.

Good thing I excel at bedroom sex.

Grinning, I round the corner from the hall, mouth already watering in anticipation of my hot cocoa and—

"Surprise!"

I jump—nearly all the way out of my skin, and whip around, mouth falling open at the sight in front of me—the kitchen full of my siblings, my parents, Bri...and Smitty and Kailey.

Frowning—mostly because I'm wondering what laws my teammate broke in order to make it here before me (or maybe what land speed records since we both left the arena at the same time)—I turn from him to the woman who owns my heart.

She's smiling and leaning back against the opposite counter. "Happy Anniversary," she says softly.

I shake my head at her, mouth curving.

Mostly because I had other plans to celebrate our anniversary.

With ice cream and pastries, books...and most importantly, *orgasms*.

None of which is all that conducive to our family surrounding us, eyes locked onto Luna and me, the mood oddly anticipatory.

I glance around again, trying to put my finger on that.

I mean, Luns makes great hot cocoa.

But it's midnight after playing a tough game against the Eagles, and...

Well, we should all be heading off to bed—and the aforementioned bedroom sex for Luns and me, to whatever else the rest of these jokers want to be doing in their own bedrooms (in their own houses, except for Bri).

Instead, everyone is standing around...*waiting*.

For what, though, I don't know.

"Bri?" Luna murmurs and I feel the energy ramp up, practically ripple through my mom and Smitty.

What the fuck?

"I got it," Bri replies softly, lifting the tray from beside Luna that I hadn't noticed before.

I see now that it's filled with enough mugs for everyone, all steaming, all filling the air with the delicious smell of hot cocoa.

Bri carries it carefully to the kitchen island, setting it between everyone.

But in front of me.

I guess they want me to pass them out?

I smother my frown, reach for the first glass, intending to give it to Luna—

And then I freeze.

Because there are letters in each the mugs—candy letters tucked into the mounds of whipped cream.

Letters that don't make sense...

Except they do when I put them all together.

Because they're spelling out:

Happy Anniversary.

And after that:

Congrats, Dad!

I turn to my dad, genuinely perplexed—especially since everyone seems to be waiting for a response from me. "Did you get a promotion or something?" I ask him.

There's silence.

Then Bri starts laughing. She turns to Luna, eyes dancing. "You called it!"

"I, um, called what?" My dad's job? I thought he was going to retire next year.

Bri shakes her head and, eyes twinkling, she starts passing out mugs. But her words are directed at Luns instead of answering my question. "I think it's time for you to go to your plan."

Luna's eyes are sparkling similarly, but she doesn't argue, just lifts a small gift bag from behind her and brings it over to me.

"What's happening?" I ask as she sets it in front of me and curls into my side.

"Open your present."

Scowling, I tug out the tissue paper, pull out the contents...

And freeze.

Because the *Congrats, Dad!* suddenly makes sense.

Fingers clenching on the edges of the book—the *baby* book —I glance down at the woman I love with everything I have in me. "Always surprising me, aren't you?"

She grins, leaning closer, settled enough in *us* that she knows this little—*huge*—surprise would never be anything but completely welcome. "I know we just started talking about kids," she says. "But apparently the universe decided it was time for us to expand our family."

Not start—because we've already done that.

The people in this room are evidence of that.

But *expand*—because love isn't contained, isn't divided, carefully portioned into bite-sized morsels.

It's infinite.

It's showing up for hot chocolate at midnight and sharing a book with a friend. It's karaoke and twinkly lights and matching rugs on the floor, standing at our sides against people who want to tear us down and filling a locker room with confetti.

It's showing up, sticking around, and being the steel wall of support as needed.

It's recognizing the gifts the universe gives us—and protecting them, keeping them safe and secure and fully in the knowledge that there's nothing they can do to decrease their value.

Because they're perfect, just as they are.

And...it's putting aside fear and thoughts of *shoulds* and *what ifs* aside in order to just be an *us*.

"I love you," I murmur, laying my hand over Luna's still flat belly.

"I know," she says. "And we"—she covers my hand with her own—"love you right back."

My heart is so full it could explode.

Luckily, it doesn't get the chance to.

"This hot chocolate is the shit!" Smitty booms.

"Language!" my mom warns him even though Bri has heard much worse, many times over.

"It's fine, Kathy," she says, right on cue.

"It's not fine! It's..."

I sigh.

Luna giggles.

But eventually the trio turns off the antics for long enough for everyone to get in on the conversation, to give Luns and me their congratulations, and to drink their hot cocoas.

It's messy and loud and filled with teasing.

It's a family.

My family.

And looking around this room, I know I wouldn't have it any other way.

Still, I can't wait for them to all leave so Luns and I can commence with *my* version of celebrating.

Because it sure as hell isn't going to involve hot cocoa.

Luna

I pad into the kitchen, pleasantly exhausted from the excitement of the night before.

Bri's joining in on the hot cocoa, coming up with the adorable idea of announcing my little—or really, *big*—surprise to Aiden and getting everyone in on the action.

And no surprise, our family showed up for us.

At midnight.

With their own lives and responsibilities and their own early mornings to get up for.

But they came anyway—because of course they did.

So, it's with a full heart that I'm walking into the kitchen, my socks silencing my footsteps as I make my way over to the coffee pot.

Bri's already left for the bakery, having the earliest morning of all of us, and I'm next up, needing to meet with Jean-Michel and Jace to give them an update on the rollout.

It's not perfect—there have been hiccups with insurance companies and legislators, confusion from patients.

But we've crossed the finish line.

Now it's just troubleshooting and working through whatever problems crop up.

And maybe planning my next way to save the world.

With Aiden and the others at my side, how can I not?

Lips turning up, I pour myself a mug of coffee and sip deeply. One per day is what my doctor recommended, so I'm going to savor it...*and* make it a really big cup.

I set it on the counter, allowing the caffeine to hit my bloodstream.

I need it.

Between the impromptu celebration with our family and then the private one Aiden and I held, just the two of us, I was up late.

Obscenely late.

And I don't care that exhaustion is clinging to my bones.

Because...I'm happy.

And I'm not alone.

And I'm not weighed down by a curse, by my father and brother—not that they've become any less annoying...they've just become less important.

As in, I don't care what they think of me.

As in, I'm not an easy target any longer—both because I've found my spine and because I've built a family who takes my back instead of trying to tear me down.

I take another sip of coffee, but this time when I set it down, I see a pile of mail that Aiden must have brought in the night before.

It looks to be three days' worth—because that was when he left for his road trip and...

Pregnancy brain strikes again.

Too bad I won't have that excuse forever.

Then I'll have to blame myself for forgetting to check the mailbox.

I sort through the pile—most of it destined for the recycling bin, but an envelope at the bottom catches my attention.

I tug it free and have to lock my knees so I don't collapse.

Because Grams's handwriting is on the front.

"What?" I whisper, hands shaking as I lift it, tear open the flap—

The paper smells like her and I hold it close to my face, inhaling the floral scent of her perfume for a long moment.

Then I start reading.

> *My baby girl,*
> *I hope you weren't too mad at me for the stunt I pulled with my will, but if this letter's reached you, it means that you've managed to fulfill my last request... and that you've done it by connecting with Aiden Black.*

I gasp, fingers crinkling the edges of the paper, eyes stinging.

Then I manage to calm myself enough and go back to reading.

> *...I know you've had a hole in your heart since you sent him away, but when I discovered he'd come home, I knew I had to find a way to push you two together...same as I knew you wouldn't seek him out, not unless you had no other choice.*
> *I'm sorry, baby.*
> *I know I overstepped, know it was too far, but as*

I write this letter, knowing that my attorney will ensure it arrives on your one year anniversary with Aiden, I know that I had to do it.

You deserve a world of peace, a life filled with love and happiness.

And you have always been good enough to be loved to obsession.

I've checked up on Aiden know he will give you that...because he needs you just as much.

I sniff again, tears escaping.

...So even though I've written other letters, I know THIS is the one that will reach you. Because I've never hoped for anything more. Because I know that you can be brave enough to do this.

Because I know you'll shatter the curse.

Because I know you'll find your great love.

Because I KNOW your life will be so full of love you won't ever even remember what it's like to be alone.

I dash at my cheeks, read the last lines.

Now live big and bright and beautiful, baby, and know that I'll be watching down on you, cheering on all your victories and sharing in all that love.

–Grams

I set the paper aside and before I can even reach for a

tissue, gentle fingers are wiping away my tears, strong arms are holding me close.

"Happy tears," Aiden says to the top of my head.

I sniff, know that I'm soaking his shirt. "Yeah, baby." Because *of course* he knows the difference.

I lift my head. "She knew."

"That you'd kick ass and save the world?" He cups my jaw. "Of course she did."

I shake my head. "She knew I'd pushed you away, knew it left a hole in me, and she knew you were playing for the Grizzlies." My mouth hitches up. "So, she decided to give me the push I needed to find you...*and* save the world."

He grins. "Never let it be said that Grams wasn't sneaky."

"And smart." I grin back. "And luckily for us, we benefited from her machinations."

"True." A beat. "And you know what else?"

I shake my head.

"We have the house to ourselves."

"Yes," I say slowly, not getting why his smile is turning wicked. "Ack!"

He scoops me up and sets me on the counter. "Which means we get to continue our celebration."

"Didn't we celebrate enough last night?

"No."

"But—"

A searing kiss that steals my breath. "Because we get to continue our celebration with kitchen sex."

Heat slices through me.

"Right," I say and because I know that the newlyweds Jean-Michel and Jace will understand precisely why I'm going to show up late for our meeting, I throw my arms around Aiden's neck and kiss him with everything I have.

"I think it's time to get me naked," I tell him as I pull back for air.

And—as usual—he doesn't disappoint me.

Gray

I spent the morning with a trio of hockey players, trying to figure out what size clothes a baby needs.

Because apparently getting newborn size isn't right.

The kid's gonna be newly born, so you think that'd make sense—to get newborn size—but apparently I know nothing.

And now, between Ryan, Smitty, and myself, we've bought more clothes than a kid needs—and then some.

And, unfortunately, I'm now aware that baby clothes come in a plethora of sizes, including the aforementioned newborn.

If only the world could see me now.

Rolling my eyes, I hit the opener, wait for the door to roll up, and then pull into the garage. I'm just popping the trunk, pulling out far too many bags of clothes when I hear my name.

That voice...

It strokes down my spine like fingers tracing nonsensical patterns over my naked flesh, moving further and further south, moving forward, rounding my body and encircling me, stroking once, twice—

I slam the trunk, turn for the house.

Know that she's going to follow me.

She always does.

And, sure enough, before my fingers reach the panel to shut the garage door, she's there, a foot behind me, floral scent in my nose.

It's intoxicating.

It's fucked up.

But that's Courtney and me—fucked up to the nth degree.

Stifling a sigh, I push into the house, walk into the kitchen, and turn around, preparing to tell her to go.

"I want a divorce."

My mouth falls open and before I can close it, she launches herself into my arms—

And kisses me.

And the worst part? I kiss her back.

Faye

I whip around, tearing my eyes from the beautiful man.

From the beautiful man *and* the woman who showed up, strolled in, and dared to kiss him with barely any preamble.

And he kissed her back.

I slant my eyes to the window above my sink again, the same window that looks right into the man's kitchen, the same window I'm standing in front of—doing dishes from my dinner for one—daydreaming about a life that isn't me waking up at home by myself. That also isn't making breakfast for myself and working at home...you guessed it, by myself. And eating lunch by myself, taking my after work walk (by myself), eating dinner, also by myself, and then bingeing whatever hot TV show is on social media until I'm too tired to stay awake—and doing it by myself.

And then—worst of all—going to sleep.

By myself.

The man picks up the beautiful woman, lifting her like she weighs nothing and setting her on the kitchen counter. Then—

"*Oh!*" I exclaim, dropping the dish I was washing and ripping my gaze away.

That's...

Well, that's a version of oral sex I've never seen before.

Heat floods my cheeks, fills my middle, flickers between my legs, and I close my eyes, count to ten.

"Stop," I whisper, slitting them open, finding that at least I didn't break the plate.

I move slowly and deliberately as I finish washing it, as I set it in the rack to dry, then repeat the process with the remaining cutlery and glass and pan that I used to sear my single chicken breast, to cook my single serving of asparagus.

I promise myself I'll give the man—the *couple*—privacy, but the sicko in me can't stop my eyes from slanting over...

Or being disappointed when I find the kitchen is empty, though the lights still blaze.

See? I'm a Peeping Tom sicko.

I shake my head, treat myself to a second glass of wine, and pad off into the living room.

I watch my show until my lids grow heavy.

Then I climb the stairs to my bedroom, wash my face, brush my teeth, and I crawl into bed.

Alone.

"Enough," I mutter to myself as I yank the covers up, as I close my eyes and deliberately clear my mind.

As I wait—a long time—for sleep to come.

But when I jerk awake what feels like minutes later, it's not to sunlight pouring into my bedroom, morning having come.

It's bright, yes.

And warm—uncomfortably so.

I sit up on a gasp...and then immediately start choking. On smoke.

Because flames are licking up the walls of my bedroom.

For once, I'm glad I'm by myself, that I'm the only one in this danger. But that flits through my mind and out of it in a flash. Because the heat is overbearing and the smoke is burning my eyes and lungs.

I finally get it together enough to throw the covers back, to drop to the floor, to start crawling for the hallway, coughing harder and harder with each foot I progress.

There's more smoke, too much smoke.

But I need to make it downstairs, need to get outside.

So, I pull my tank top up, getting a bit of relief from the smoke, and keep crawling.

Then I'm in the hall, turning to the right, searching the flickering blackness for the stairs—

"Ow!" I cry out as I tumble headfirst down several steps, having found them in the least helpful way.

Falling.

My face hurts and my wrist is screaming, but I know I can't stop.

Not when it seems to be getting hotter by the second, hotter than anything I've ever felt.

Not when it's getting harder and harder to breathe with each passing moment.

Not when I can—literally—see my life flashing before my eyes.

I keep half-crawling and half-falling down the stairs, crashing hard onto the landing and trying to orient myself.

But I can't see anything.

And I can't breathe.

Weakness seeps into my legs, my arms, the shirt not protecting me any longer, the heat and smoke closing in. It's so dark, so disorienting, and I don't know where the front door is, don't know how to get out, don't know how to do this...

By myself.

But just as those words slide through my mind, as my arms give way and I crumple to the floor—

The front door bursts open in a splintering of wood, a shattering of glass.

MARRIED TO NUMBER 22   273

And the last thing I see before black sucks me under...
Is the man from next door.

THANK YOU FOR READING! I hope you love Aiden and Luna's story as much as I do! The next book in the Grizzlies Hockey series is DIVORCED FROM NUMBER THIRTY-EIGHT. **He's the man of my dreams—and only my dreams —until he bursts through my front door...and doesn't leave.**
CLICK HERE TO READ DIVORCED FROM NUMBER THIRTY-EIGHT NOW>

AND IN THE MEANTIME, do you want more than a taste of those yummy Eagles hockey players? **Once lucky, twice shy. Three times...and I might claim a sexy hockey player as my own. Read** LUCKY LACES now.

IF YOU ENJOY MY SERIES, considering supporting me on PATREON! Get access to early releases, bonus content, character art, audiobooks, special edition covers, swag, and much more!

CLICK HERE TO SUPPORT ME>

GRIZZLIES HOCKEY

Married to Number Twenty-Two
Divorced from Number Thirty-Eight
Knocked Up by Number Ninety

Hate missing Elise's new releases? Love contests, exclusive excerpts and giveaways?
Then signup for Elise's newsletter here!

www.elisefaber.com/newsletter

And join Elise's fan group, the Fabinators (https://www.facebook.com/groups/fabinators) for insider information, sneak peaks at new releases, and fun freebies! Hope to see you there!

If you enjoy my series, considering supporting me on PATREON! Get access to early releases, bonus content, character art, audiobooks, special edition covers, swag, and much more!

CLICK HERE TO SUPPORT ME>

I so appreciate your help in spreading the word about my books, including sharing with friends! Please leave a review on your favorite book site!

ALSO BY ELISE FABER

Broken

Boldly

Breathless

Ballsy

Bewitched

Blowout

Breathe

Blazed

Sierra Hockey Series

Over the Line

Caught from Behind

The Big Skate

On the Fly

Eagles Hockey Series (all stand alone)

Broken Laces

Lace 'em Up

Knotted Laces

Loaded Laces

Lucky Laces

Oak Ridge Vineyards

Bottles & Blades

Beauty & the Boardroom

The Bachelor & the Break-in

Rush Hockey Trilogy #1

Big Puck Energy

Filthy Puckboy

So Pucking Over It

Rush Hockey Trilogy #2

Love, Pucks, and Other Stories

All's Fair in Pucks and War

No Pucks Lost Between Us

Rush Hockey Novellas

Puck and Make Up

Billionaire's Club (**all stand alone**)

Bad Night Stand

Bad Breakup

Bad Husband

Bad Hookup

Bad Divorce

Bad Fiancé

Bad Boyfriend

Bad Blind Date

Bad Wedding

Bad Engagement

Bad Bridesmaid

Bad Swipe

Bad Girlfriend

Bad Best Friend

Bad Rebound

Bad Romance

Bad Business

Bad Billionaire's Quickies

Love, Action, Camera (all stand alone)

Dotted Line

Action Shot

Close-Up

End Scene

Meet Cute

Love After Midnight (all stand alone)

Rum And Notes

Virgin Daiquiri

On The Rocks

Sex On The Seats

Life Sucks Series

Train Wreck

Hot Mess

Dumpster Fire

Clusterf*@k

FUBAR

Perfect Storm

Free Fall

Lost Cause

Roosevelt Ranch Series (all stand alone, series complete)

Disaster at Roosevelt Ranch

Heartbreak at Roosevelt Ranch

Collision at Roosevelt Ranch

Regret at Roosevelt Ranch

Desire at Roosevelt Ranch

Phoenix Series (read in order)

Phoenix Rising

Dark Phoenix

Phoenix Freed

Phoenix: LexTal Chronicles (rereleasing soon, stand alone, Phoenix world)

From Ashes

In Flames

To Smoke

KTS Series (all stand alone, series complete)

Riding The Edge

Crossing The Line

Leveling The Field

Scorching The Earth

Cocky Heroes World

Tattooed Troublemaker

ABOUT THE AUTHOR

USA Today bestselling author, Elise Faber, loves chocolate, Star Wars, Harry Potter, and hockey (the order depending on the day and how well her team -- the Sharks! -- are playing). She and her husband also play as much hockey as they can squeeze into their schedules, so much so that their typical date night is spent on the ice. Elise is the mom to two exuberant boys and lives in Northern California. Connect with her in her Facebook group, the Fabinators or find more information about her books at www.elisefaber.com.

facebook.com/elisefaberauthor

amazon.com/author/elisefaber

bookbub.com/profile/elise-faber

instagram.com/elisefaber

tiktok.com/@elisefaberauthor

goodreads.com/elisefaber